Chris Steadman Presents…

A Generation One Story

IT'S TIME FOR A NEW FIGHTING CHAMPION!!!

LET THE FIGHTING BEGIN!!!

IT'S TIME TO SCRAP!!!

Chapter 1. One Mission

"You messed up. You know you messed up right?", my friend Jamal tells me.

I have gotten myself into a beef, I guess, with some guy named Michael, or "No Games", his gang name. To be honest, I forgot how it happened. Something about me liking his girl's picture on Instagram and commenting on it. I may or may not have tried to shoot my shot with her, but at the time I thought she was single.

He responded talking tough, so I returned with tough talk myself. He threatened me, saying he'll beat me up and shoot and stuff, but I've known him since 3rd grade. He's built a reputation for talking tough but not doing anything, so I wasn't sweating it. I've tried to forget about it, but with Jamal in my ear, it's kind of hard.

"Today is Friday and he said him and the rest of his gang will pull up when school is out. What did you do!?", he asks.

"All I did was like Stacy's picture on Instagram. I didn't know she dated a gang member.", I tell him.

"Well, what are you going to do?", he asks.

"Um... I don't know, and I really don't want to think about it. I got better stuff to worry about.", I tell him.

"Well you better, or that's your ass or possibly your life! I'll talk to you after lunch."

As I walked to class, I see Stacy walk by me. She looked like she wanted to tell me something, but she kept on walking. She seemed like she was in a rush but wanted to warn me about something. I don't sweat it though and wave and smile at her.

She ignores me and keeps on walking. I get a feeling of disappointment, but mostly anger. She's the one who has been entertaining me this long and we've been texting for three months now. No Games should be mad at her, not me. I didn't even know she was in a relationship till recent.

I walk to my first period class and as the teacher starts her lesson, I zone all the way out. I can see and feel people looking at me though. It's probably because they know about the beef. I even hear some talking about it, but I zone them out too.

With all this happening on Sunday, I had forgotten all about this. With me working to help my mom and my sister, foolish things like this slip my mind and honestly, I think he's bluffing. I go through the rest of my first period class and once again, I totally forget all about it by 3rd period. I try to focus on what I'm going to do before I clock in at work today.

School goes by and I was supposed to meet up with Jamal after lunch, but he had restriction for skipping 2nd period and ate his lunch in the gym. He stayed there for the rest of the day. He spots me though as I walk home from school and catches up to me. He starts talking fast and franticly.

"Aye bro! We have to move fast before they pull up. Some kid in restriction told me No Games not tryna talk, and he got heat!", he tells me franticly.

"What? Bruh it's not that serious. He's probably capping too.", I say trying to laugh it off, thinking he's joking.

"No bro! He showed me the pictures! They not playing today!", he says in a panic.

"Wait, you saw the pictures of them with the guns?", I ask starting to get a little bit worried.

"Yea bro, we gotta go now!"

I wasn't worried before, but now I feel my heart drop when he confirms that he saw a pictures with them with guns. I really don't want to believe him, but I can't take the chance of them actually pulling up on me right now. We both plan to dash home as soon as possible.

We look around and make sure no one is on to us. Then we slowly speed up more and more until we were almost fully sprinting. My house is kind of far away from the school in walking distance. I don't have a car and usually don't mind the walk, but today is obviously different.

We almost make it to my house when we suddenly hear a loud skirt and engine roar down the street. A red 1988 Hyundai Excel. I feel my heart start to beat faster and faster. I know it's them. We try to run faster, but it does us no good at all.

They catch up to us and three of them in the back seat jump out the car to grab us. We try to struggle them off but fail. Two more of them jumped out the car.

"Which one of you is "MoneymakerJoseph?", No Games asks.

Jamal instantly points to me. I was mad at him for a second, but then I saw the fear in his eyes and couldn't blame him. He had nothing to do with this and was just trying to help me get home in time and avoid them.

They throw him on the ground and put me up against a brick apartment projects.

"So, it's yo punk ass talking bout my girl on Instagram huh. Well what's good now punk!", says No Games.

I want to talk trash back at him, but I know it could lead to even more drama. It's more of them, and only me and Jamal. I bite my tongue hard and ball up my fist as they hold me to the wall.

But my efforts to lower the hostility of course failed.

I see one of them pull a gun out and holds it by his hip.

At this point I knew it was not a game and they were serious, but sadly it may be a little too late.

I knew I was going to die, over nothing.

"Please don't kill him! It's not that serious!", Jamal cried.

"Shut up! You better leave before it be two dead bodies I catch today!", No Games says.

No Games pulls out a gun and pulls the clip. I began to struggle for my life and cry thinking it's over. I'm not short or too small, but No Games stands at about 6'6 while I'm only six feet tall.

He suddenly stops though and looks down the street. We hear a car with loud bass drive fast down the street. A red 2008 Impala SS with shiny 22-inch blade rims pulls up and parks in front of the project apartments. I can't see who's inside though due to the heavy tint. Six more Blood gang members get out the car.

"Aye No Games! Chill yo ass out mane!", one of them say while getting out the car.

A guy who seems to be the leader approaches No Games and takes his gun.

"Nah he was the one talking bout Stacy and talking crazy on Instagram. All on my girls page!", No Game says.

"Ion know why you care about that gal anyways, plus we done already dropped 3 fools this week already and word is that twelve is on us cuz someone snitched! We need to chill fool!", the leader says.

"Ight, but I'm gonna at least whoop his ass then!"

"Well do that then."

They throw me hard on the ground. "Get up! Let's scrap punk!", No Games tells me.

I know I'm not getting out of this, so I get up and put my hands into a fist. Growing up in Memphis taught me how to fight. I've been in many already, but it's kind of normal around here, and I'm not that small so I know how to defend myself. But they circle around me so it's getting jumped that I'm worried about.

He swings a punch, but I duck under him and jab him twice in the face. He stumbles back a little.

"Oh so you can move huh, ight bet!", he tells me chuckling afterwards.

As we square up more and size each other up, I punch him one more time on the side of his face. It hurts my hand badly, but I see him stumble again and he falls back against the Impala. I give him no time to recover, and I run up on him swinging and hitting him in the face and his body with all I got, yelling in the process.

But then suddenly, I feel two hands on my shoulders and instantly know it's over for me. They slam me back to the ground, and I fall headfirst on the sidewalk. I hear a loud ringing noise in my head and before I knew it, I was getting jumped.

They stomp and kick me and start to yell and cuss at me.

I get kicked in the ribs and let out a loud, painful yell. "Shut up! You ain't so tuff no more huh!", says No Games.

"Chill! Chill! You got it! I'm sorry! I'm sorry! Stop it!", I cry and plead for them to do. But not shockingly, they ignore me. I get jumped for at least four minutes straight, but it feels like four years.

"Aye No Games, lets bounce.", the leader finally says.

"Ight!", No Games says.

Before they leave, No Games kicks me dead in the eye. I yell in pain even more.

"Next time watch how you talk to people fool! Next time we won't be so nice!", No Games tells me as I groan and cry on the ground.

I hear them all take off in their cars. I can't open my eye and it even hurts to cry, but I do. Jamal approaches me slowly and helps me up.

"I'm sorry bro.", he says, then he begins to cry too.

He asks me do I want to go to the hospital, but I tell him I can't miss work. As crazy as that sounds, that's how bad my situation is at home with money.

He argues with me to go but I convince him after telling him my mom took health science classes in college and she can help me. He walks me to my house and as we do, people look and stare. Some of them knew what happened and some even shake their heads in sadness. But they don't do or didn't do anything to stop it. Everyone is afraid of the gangs around here, and nobody trusts the police to actually do anything about it.

We make it to my house, dab up, and he leaves.

I walk in my room, and I know my mom will be worried when she sees me. She gets home when I'm at work so I should be good for now. I don't want to let my problems interfere with our daily routine. My sister is home though on the phone with her friend, so I rush to my room, so she doesn't see my eye.

"Hey Joseph, you can at least speak before you rush to your room.", she says.

"Sorry I'm late for work!", I tell her.

She hears our dog barking and leaves my door. It's our big pit-bull. We named him Bishop, after 2pac's character in Juice. He's the sweetest dog but he will defend his family to the death. I wish he was there with me earlier, even though sadly, they probably would have shot him.

I look in my mirror and try to open my eye. I yell in pain as I do, and I only keep it open for a second. When I do manage to keep it open long enough to see it, I see it's bloodshot red and it feels very dry, and it burns. I close it and grab a rag and let it soak in cold water and put it on my eye. As I change clothes I see my ribs, very bruised and purplish and it even hurts to breathe.

I rush as fast as I possibly can out the door before my sister sees me. Hopefully my eye heals a little bit before I'm off work. As for my ribs, I'll have to walk it off for now. We can't afford a day missed from work. We need as many hours as we can get. We're very poor and have no close family in Memphis. The closest family we have are in Nashville and they're poor too.

To be honest, I would've dropped out of school to work, but my mom insists that I go to college, knowing good and well we can't afford that and I'm not smart enough to get a scholarship. Me and my mom bud heads every now and then, but it's only because we want what's best for each other. I just hope she doesn't lose it when she finds out what happened. Word spreads around Memphis quickly, so I know she'll find out eventually.

I walk into Kroger 20 minutes late. You would think I would be pissed or upset about the fight, which I am a little, but I'm madder about being late to work. My manager Jax walks up to me.

"You good Joseph?", he asks.

"Yea, everything's fine, why?" Honestly, I don't know if he's asking because I'm never late or because my eye.

"Your eye looks swollen." Well there's my answer.

"Oh, I got into a little scrap that's all. I'm fine though.", I say to him lying.

"Oh, ok. Let me know if you need anything, ok?"

"Ok."

I go to the restroom, walking past all of my coworkers awkwardly, to look at my eye. It's giant! There is no way I can hide this from my mom, or even people at school.

As if things couldn't get worse, my phone blows up from notifications out of nowhere. I look on my phone and see my named mentioned a lot on Instagram. I click to open the notification. On one slide of the post, it's a video of me getting jumped. My face instantly goes red. A mixture of embarrassment and anger flows through my body. Especially with me knowing I was beating his ass before I got jumped.

I scroll to the second slide and it's a message saying, "We ain't done wit you yet!". I feel a tight, sick feeling in my stomach. At first, earlier today, I wasn't worried, but now knowing that they ain't playing, I'm even scared to leave this restroom.

They could pull up on me anytime. I wish I could call the cops, but they make things worse. And after what happened to me as a child, I'll never ever call them even if Michael Myers were stalking me. They never seem to arrest the actual bad guys.

This is just hell. My ribs, my eye, my head, money, and this sickness in my stomach because of No Games! It's all too much! I want to crack but if I do then I'll let my mom and sister down. I don't know…… It's just hard to survive out here. I guess I'll have to try to finish work for the day without thinking about all this.

I go back and start to stock food. Surprisingly enough, Jamal walks in. He dabs me up and I guess tries to cheer me up.

"Bruh, you actually know how to fight. Before you got jumped, you were beating his ass.", he tells me trying to make me feel better.

It doesn't work.

"Well yea, but that doesn't matter cuz I still got my ass beat.", I tell him. I'm not going to tell him about the video, but he'll probably find out soon. He then starts to rant on about a fighting tournament or something, I really don't know. I start to zone out and can only hear him blabbering on and on.

As I zone out and look past him out the window, I see the same red Impala from earlier.

My heart suddenly drops into my stomach yet again. I try not to panic in front of Jamal, but I hope they don't come in here to find me.

"Are you even listening to me Joseph?", he says frustrated. I don't want to warry him, or possibly get him jumped and beat up as well, so I don't tell him about the Impala outside.

"My bad bro, look I got to get to work before I get in trouble. I'll catch up with you later, ok?", I tell him still looking outside.

"Ight bro.", he response.

As he exits, the Impala leaves the parking lot, relieving me for a moment. I also see Jamal get into the car with his big brother Larry, so I know he's good and won't get caught walking home.

A few seconds after that, I see the police also drive around the parking lot, explaining why the Impala left. They were trying to get away from the cops, but hopefully they didn't spot me here. I try to clear my mind and finish my shift.

I clock out and wave all my co-workers goodbye. It's 11:00pm so it's pitch-black dark. I'm even more spooked. I've spent all day stocking watching my back, jumping every time someone called my name.

As I walk home, I start to feel my ribs and eye and they still hurt like hell. It's very dark out and the more I walk, the more pain I feel. I lie down slowly holding my ribs, grunting and crying, and I try not to breathe too hard.

And as if my life couldn't get worse, I see bright lights beaming down the street and get the strong sense that it's the red Impala.

I was correct.

I get up and limp away as fast as I can, looking very pitiful. They catch up to me of course and they get out the car. Of course No Games is here, plus the guy I think is their leader and four others.

"Sup punk.", says No Games. "We ain't done wit yo ass yet."

"What do ya'll want!?", I say scarily. I try to hold back my tears back but they come out.

"Stop crying bitch!", says the leader. We ain't come to fight right now. But you ain't out yo debt either. We need more from you."

"Debt?", I say. "What you mean debt man?"

"My name ain't man, it's Red Angel. And that ass beating wasn't enough. Me and my bruddas ain't satisfied so we need more. And that more is money."

"Look man… I mean… Red Angel, I'm broke.", I tell them.

"Oh I know you are, but we saw you at yo job. We know you know where the money at too.", he says.

"You want me to steal from my own job? I can't do that, I'll go to jail, there's gotta be something else.", I beg.

"I mean, we could beat your ass again, or kill you right here right now. The choice is really yours.", he tells me. I look around and learn from my mistake from last time. I know they aren't messing around.

"So what's it gonna be?", No Games asks.

"I'll do it." , I say desperately with no other rational choice it seems.

"Good, now have it in 24 hours and meet us behind the tennis court. Have the money or, well, you know.", Red Angel says.

They laugh and mock me then they all hop back into the Impala. I sit down and realize what I've done.

I've messed up badly. It's really crazy how one Friday could change my life forever. I can't even come to terms of what just happened and what I have to do tomorrow.

And at this point, I wouldn't be surprised if I died soon.

I finally make it home. Everyone is sleep and I see my mom's work jacket on the couch, so I know she's home. Me coming home late or while she's sleep is normal, so I'm not really worried about that. It's my injuries that I'm worried about her seeing. I go weeks without seeing my mom sometimes due to our tight schedule, so I should be fine for now. It's tomorrow I'm scared about. I've never stole anything a day in my life and now I have to steal from my own job that I've worked at for four years now, or else I'll die or at least get hurt badly again. I try to get some sleep and worry about it tomorrow.

As I fall asleep, I have weird images pull up in my head. I wouldn't necessarily call them dreams, because it's everything that's happened so far. Me commenting on Stacy's post, me and Jamal running, me getting jumped, me jumping at work whenever someone called my name or me constantly looking over my shoulder, and me meeting with them after work. I even see things that haven't happened yet. Me getting arrested, and me getting killed by Red Angel and No Games. I constantly wake up in a sweat in the middle of the night, and I try to force myself back to sleep.

I wake up and where I'm usually happy on Saturday mornings, all the weight hits me back in my chest. I have to clock in at 10:00 in the morning. My sister is still sleep but as I walk in the kitchen the pain hits again. It feels like I've been hurt forever now, but it only just happened yesterday.

I try to sneak out the house without waking anyone up but I guess Bishop, who is in my sister's room, heard me walking down the hall to the living room. He starts barking and whining to get to me. He probably needs to go out and use it, but I don't have time. I hear my sister get up and I rush out the door as fast as I possibly can.

I walk down the street and eventually go to the park and sit at a bench.

"What am I going to do?", I say to myself as I put my hands on my face. I sit and just listen to the kids playing, birds chirping, and remember how simple life used to be when I was a kid. Honestly, it seems everything changed after my dad died.

He was murdered by a police officer during a traffic stop right in front of me and my mother. My sister, Savannah, was too young to remember. After that, my mom had to drop out of her classes in college to support me and my sister. It was a big riot and I remember everyone going crazy. My mom was on TV a couple times and people took care of us for a while. Then I guess the hype died down and people just forgot about us.

I don't care about all that though. I only care about the memories I have with my dad. Us playing basketball, playing my GameCube, or him reading the Bible to me. Honestly, I don't think I've been happy since his death.

I sit and reminisce for about 15 minutes, but then suddenly, I feel someone tap my shoulder.

I look up and see a pretty black girl with four very long pigtail braids in each corner of her head, so long that they go past her knees.

"Um, sorry, do you know where I can find…". She looks at a piece of paper.

"Master Isaiah?"

"Um, no, I've never heard that name before.", I tell her. I stutter a little bit because I'm not going to lie, she's fine.

"Ugh, ok, thanks.", she says.

"Um, no problem.", I say sounding awkward as hell.

Her paper falls out her hands and blows in the wind.

"Damn it.", she says. She doesn't run to grab it, but she uses her braids and they reach far enough to grab it. I sit and watch in amazement.

"Woah!", I say out loud. I immediately regret it due to embarrassment.

She smiles at me and says goodbye and walks away.

With all this extra stuff going on I totally forgot that powers exist. Not everyone has them but a good majority do. I remember being a little kid and praying every night that my power would come, but I never got it. And in the ghetto, I can't sit and hope I get superpowers like a video game or a comic book. I have to survive and help my family.

I have to clock in about an hour from now and I start to plan how I'm going to do this.

I think I'm going to take the money towards the end of my shift. That way I can give it straight to Red Angel and not have to hold it. It's going to be easier said than done, but what choice do I have.

An hour goes by and I'm finally at work. Jax and the others greet me as usual. I feel so fake greeting them back knowing the crime I have to commit to the people who trust me. Who hired me at 14. People I call my second family. But still, what choice do I have.

3:00pm comes around and I go on my lunch break. I'm sweating as the time gets closer and closer. I take a seat in the breakroom and look on my phone. I see my phone has been blown up with messages from my mom.

"WHY DIDN'T YOU TELL ME AND WHAT HAPPENED!!!", the message reads from my mom. She sends me a video of the fight. I knew she would find out, but damn that was fast.

I look up and hear two of my co-workers, Frank and Derrick, talking about something and they both seem very excited about it.

"It's almost time! I can't wait!", says Frank.

"Who do you have your money on?", asked Derrick.

" Mr. USA, duh! The strongest man on the planet."

"I don't know, Austin U.K. isn't bad and he has been showing his power on social media lately. It's even been on the news."

"What's water going to do to muscle, huh Derrick?", Frank says.

"What are ya'll talking about?", I ask interrupting their conversation.

"The Time to Scrap Tournament Joseph, the biggest world event ever.", Franks says like I should already know.

"Even bigger than the Olympics", Derrick says.

"Oh I think I've heard of that before when I was younger, it's been a long time though. Isn't that for like people born with powers to fight and see who is the best?"

"Yea, well, one person won once who wasn't born with powers before.", Derrick tells me.

"Really? Who?", I ask.

Frank then says with a lot of energy, " The GOAT, Master Isaiah!"

I get a confused, shocked look on my face. Then it hits me. That's the name that pretty girl said earlier. Why was she looking for him? Is she going to enter the tournament? And why is he in Memphis?

"How did he win without powers?", I ask.

"Well other than him mastering his own street fighting style mixed with a little bit of martial arts fighting style he called Scrap Arts, he developed his own power called Ze.", Derrick explains.

"Ze?", I asked confused. "That sounds dumb."

"Well it worked, and that's how he won the first tournament in 1987. That's why he's known as the GOAT.", Frank says.

Derrick interrupts, "But to be fair, he lost the second one in 91' to Master Jiro from Japan, who also used Ze. And since then people with powers learned how to use their power even better, so Ze became pretty much useless."

"Who won last time?", I ask.

"Mr. USA duh, which is why he's going to win this year!", Franks says.

"Sure Frank.", Derrick says sarcastically.

"Don't be a hater Derrick, where is your American pride? And he's going to bring that $5,000,000 back to America again."

"Wait, $5,000,000! That's how much you'll get if you win?", I say with excitement and disbelief.

"Yep, can set someone up for life. Even generations.", Derrick tells me.

Hell, with all I'm dealing with, I could use $5,000,000.

Our lunch break ends and we exit the breakroom onto the floor and get back to work.

One more hour left until my shift is over. I still remember my mission and know what I have to do. First I need to get into Jax's office to cut off the cameras. Then go to what we call, "the money room", where they take and count the register money. I'll need to wait till Jax walks out though.

I stand by a register waiting for him to exit his office. My heart beating hard and the sweat dripping from my arm pits down my body makes this more tense than I want it to be. He finally exits. It's time.

I move, not fast but swiftly to his door. I look around to make sure it's clear and then enter the office. I shut the door and see the monitor with different camera angles inside and outside the store and approach it. Then suddenly, it hits me.

A giant apple, swollen feeling hits my throat. My heart beats rapidly, and I'm breathing so hard that it's causing major pain to my ribs and I can hear myself breathing. And the sweat dripping from my forehead to my eye makes this worse as well.

"I can't do this!", I say to myself. I'm not a criminal . I can't steal from my people. They are just going to have to jump me, or kill me, because I can't do this. I walk out Jax's office and finish my shift, coming to terms that this could be my last day alive.

My shift ends and I exit the building. I wonder should I just go to the tennis court to tell them and try to beg and plead for my life, or just run home. That's an easy choice and I decide to run home. I figure they'll kill me either way. Although me running home isn't really me running because my ribs hurt like hell, so it's really just a weak limp.

My job is closer to my house than my school is but it's still like 15 minutes away walking distance. I make some progress but my ribs and eye still hurt like hell, but I try to force my way home. I get slower, and slower as time goes by.

I take turns jogging and running as fast as I possibly can. Suddenly, bright lights appear once again, and I instantly know it's on. They turn their high beams on so now it's even brighter and they honk the horn a lot. I can hear No Games yelling in the car even from down the street.

"Damn it!", I say to myself.

The car speeds down the road but I split between two buildings down an alley. I hear them hop out and say get his ass. I have a little head start and at this point I forget about my ribs and run very fast. I'm going off of pure adrenaline at this point. I'm running for my life.

I keep on running but I see a brick wall in front of me. I know if I don't make it over the wall on time, it'll be over for me. I struggle to get on top of a trash can, but they start to catch up to me. Like close enough to where I can clearly see them as I struggle over the wall. I get over the brick wall at the last second, but they don't give up and get over the wall too.

They could have shot me right then and there, but they kept on chasing. That lets me know that they want to jump me again so I can feel the pain. And hell, they might shoot me anyways after they jump me.

It starts pouring rain and I slip a couple times but recover quickly. However, I hit a dead end in the back alley with nowhere to go but backwards.

They catch up to me.

"You think we're stupid don't you? Like we didn't think this would happen.", Red Angel says.

"Please bruh! Please let me go!", I plead.

"Couldn't, even if I wanted to. Get him.", he commands the others.

They walk up to me and I prepare to protect my face as they approach me.

"HEY!"

Everyone pauses as a loud hey can be heard. They turn around and I see it's the girl from earlier with the hair power and a middle-aged man. He seems fit though and is wearing a black jumpsuit with gold stripes on the side. He's bald but has a thick grey goatee on his face.

"Who the hell are ya'll? Get the hell out of here before ya'll get hurt too!", No Games says.

"I think it's you all that should leave.", says the man.

He doesn't raise his voice but says it so sternly that it even sends chills down my spine. He really meant it. But No Games really meant what he said too I guess and pulls out a gun.

"Nia!", the man yells.

The girl does two flips and jumps in the air doing a backflip, and like earlier, grabs the gun with her hair while in the air.

"What the?", says No Games shocked.

"Aye yo! They got powers. Back off!", Red Angel commanded.

"Nah, forget that, get her!', No Games says.

The others hesitate but in pure rage, No Games runs up to the girl and tries to punch her, but she catches his wrist with her hair and throws him over her all while standing still. He lands on his back hard and yells and groan in pain.

"Wasn't very smart huh?", she says.

They help him up and they all walk away. They all mean mug me as they walk past me, but Red Angel says something before he leaves.

"They ain't gonna be here to protect you forever! Yo debt ain't paid for either and it just got deeper!", he threatens.

They walk off and the girl walks up to me.

"Hey, it's you from earlier. You ok?", she asks.

"No.", I say. All the adrenaline is gone and all the pain hits me ten times harder. I fall to the ground and let out a loud cry as I hold my ribs.

"Master Isaiah, can you help him?", the girl asks.

"Not much I can do but take him to the hospital.", he says.

"Good idea.", she replies. She picks me up and carries me in her arms. As she carries me, I fade away, falling asleep in pain.

Chapter 2. Train Me

I finally wake up and I look around to see I'm in a hospital bed. I look to the left and see the girl and the man, and on my right I see my sister.

"He's up!", my sister says happily.

"Good.", the man says. Him and the girl gets up and starts to walk away.

"Wait!", I say before they walk out the room. I now know that this is Master Isaiah, the first Time to Scrap Tournament winner. I have to ask him, or at least see.

"Um, thank you.", I say awkwardly.

"Oh, no problem. I know it's crazy out here. Try to stay safe.", he says.

I call out again, "No wait, um… are you Master Isaiah? The first Time to Scrap Tournament winner?"

He gets a serious look on his face and asks, "Can I help you?", he asks sternly again.

"Um yea, I know and heard how good you are. And that you weren't born with powers."

"Get on with it kid.", he rushes.

"Can you train me? Please! So I can enter the Time to Scrap Tournament.", I say rushing to the point.

"Are you crazy!?", my sister says.

"Yea, I think he is!", the girl agrees.

"Sorry kid, I don't just offer my services to everybody. Plus, the Time to Scrap Tournament isn't just a joke or for people to just get fame or a country battle. It's a serious fight and you'll probably die trying to fight super people.", the man says.

"No you have it all wrong. Plus you can teach me how to use Ze like someone did for you.", I say. He gets a slight surprise look on his face, but smirks.

"You can't just get Ze or teach it kid, but I see you obviously have done your research on me, good job.", he says.

"Please sir! I really need the money!", I beg.

"Why? For your little debt?", he says.

"What debt?", my little sister asks in concern.

"Well it may be little to you but it's my life for me. Plus I need it for me, my sister, and my momma.", I tell him.

I look around and it hits me that my mom isn't here. I know she works a lot, but I know if she knows I'm at the hospital, which she does because my sister is here, she would be here.

"Wait, where is she?", I ask my sister.

"Well…… she got sick.", she tells me.

"What do you mean she got sick?", I ask frantically.

"I was going to tell you once you got home, she passed out when she got home from work and had a high fever. I called the ambulance and they took her to the hospital. She refused to stay and she didn't want to call you to disturb your work and make you panic. Then they called me from your phone and told me what happened to you. ", she explains.

"Mom is sick….", I start to panic.

If she gets too ill, or die, our life will really be hell. We both been holding back our personal issues for so long that now both of us are in pain, physically and mentally. I know she's going through hell too because she found out what happened to me yesterday, and now she's sick.

"Please! It's my only way-out sir! I need this for me and my family. I won't disappoint you I promise!", I beg.

I can tell he starts to think about it. He stares at me, then my sister, and then at me again. He then looks at the ground.

"You know, I'm going to push you past your mental and physical limits. And you'll have to stay with me, so forget about school.", he tells me.

"I don't care just please give me a chance!", I beg again.

He thinks again for a second.

"Fine.", he replies.

"What!?", both the girl and my sister say in shock.

"You're kidding me right!?", says the girl.

"Be at 419 Grove Ln at 6:00am tomorrow, not a second late.", he tells me.

"Tomorrow? But my ribs are still in pain and my eye…"

"Hey!", he interrupts. He yells loudly and it sends echoes in the room. He then asks me a question. "You want to win and not waste my time right!?"

"Well yea."

"Then be there, if you want to help your family. I'm giving you a chance. Don't waste my time.", he says.

"Yes sir, thank you."

They both leave the room. The girl walks away in disbelief.

"So you think the best way you can support us is this tournament? What the hell are you thinking!?", my sister says.

"Look if I lose, we'll just be in the same spot we're in now. If I win, we'll have $5,000,000. I'll take my chances. It's not like the NBA or the NFL. It's fighting, something I'm already pretty damn good at. Plus if he can give me the power he had, I may actually stand a chance.", I explain. I may be underestimating this, but damn, what options do I honestly have. It seems like the only light I have in this dark place.

"Fine, can you at least talk to mom about it first?", my sister asks.

"Sure."

Later that night we call out the hospital, ignoring the doctor's recommendations. My sister helps me home and as we walk in the door, I see our mom on the couch.

"Hey baby, you ok?", she asks. I expected her to be angry because of the video or upset, but she sounds more exhausted, just like me. Not like sleepy, but just tired of this rough life.

She gets up and hugs me and helps me sit on the couch. She starts coughing. "Joseph, look baby if you want me to call the police I will."

"No momma, I'm good. Are you ok?"

"Well, I've been better. They saying I shouldn't go to work anymore but you know me, so we'll see how that'll go."

"Momma please…", my sister interrupts.

"Savannah don't start right now; I'm not doing this again." She starts to cough again. "You know I have to work."

"But Joseph is going to enter a fighting tournament for $5,000,000.", Savannah says, spoiling the news.

"The hell?", my mom says trying to catch her breath. I can tell she almost got a heart attack just from hearing that.

"Boy what you getting into? Don't let that gang get you in trouble or kicked out this house."

"No momma, I'm entering the Time to Scrap Tournament.", I tell her.

"Really? I've heard of that before. That started around the time I was a kid. How you gonna win without any powers? And what happens if you get hurt?", she asks.

I'm being trained by the first winner of the tournament, and he also wasn't born with powers. I talked to him while I was out today.", I tell her.

"You talking about Isaiah?", she asks.

I get shocked that she knows of him.

"Yea, how do you know him?", I ask.

"He was a celebrity in the 80's and 90's for winning it. He was the first winner and it was a big deal because he was black. We as black people looked up to him. He was like Michael Jordan. But after the pressure and America hating him, he kind of faded away. He planned to make a comeback the next tournament but he lost."

"Yea, I've heard. Only shtick is I have to stay there until the tournament.", I tell her.

"Well it sounds good to me. When does training start?", she says. I'm surprised she's actually entertaining the idea. But I think she views it like me. It can't get any worse than it is now and only good can happen, like winning the prize money.

"Tomorrow.", I tell her.

"Oh that's sooner than I thought. As long as you don't get hurt too badly, I'll support you baby."

"Thanks momma. I won't let neither of you down.", I promise them. Bishop comes running in and jumps up on me and starts licking me.

"You too Bishop.", I say trying to get him off of me. We all laugh and head to bed.

As I get in my bed, I start to feel a little feeling of hope in my soul again. Maybe this can be the turnaround in life I've been waiting for. It's crazy how things in life can change so fast.

The morning comes and I pack my stuff. My momma has cooked breakfast for me before I leave. After breakfast she offers to drive me but I walk instead to get a little warm up in. I leave early to make sure no one will be out, like Red Angel or No Games. I leave at 5:30am to save myself some time.

As I walked out though, I couldn't help but to think about Red Angel. Now if they do find me, it's instantly death. Even if I lose this tournament, hopefully I could defend myself if they do try to jump me and maybe even others in my community.

I show up at the address at 5:59am. I knock on the door, but no one answers. I knock for about two minutes. I start to think he lied to me and I get frustrated, but before I knock again I'm suddenly swept from my feet and next thing I know I'm being hanged upside down by my feet.

"What the?", I say.

"See, you don't even keep your guard up at all times."

It's the girl with hair powers. She's hanging me with her hair wrapped around my feet.

"I wasn't ready!", I say getting dizzy and mad.

"That's my point. You should always be ready at all times!", she tells me.

"Easy for you to say Rapunzel!", I say. She drops me on my head and it hurts like hell.

"My name is Nia and you better watch yourself before I kick your ass!"

"HEY!"

It's Master Isaiah and he finally answers the door.

"Both of you hush! Now get in here before I kick both of your asses!"

Chapter 3. First Day In

We both walk in his house. It's not too big but it's a nice size for it to be in Memphis. He gives us a little tour of the place. He says we will do most of our training in his backyard and his basement. His backyard is surrounded by a tall brick wall he built himself. It is also a nice size. His basement is pretty big too. It holds his medal from the first tournament.

"How was it like? The first tournament?", I ask.

"It was life changing. No one really knew what to expect at the time. It definitely didn't have the hype like it does now though.", he says.

"But after word got around that a guy with no powers won the damn thing, people couldn't believe it."

"Must've been crazy.", Nia says.

"Yeah, but they used it as a sign that maybe regular people can be just as important and special as people with powers. I didn't care about all that though, I only cared about taking care of my family, just like you…..", he pauses, searching for my name.

"Joseph.", I answer.

"Yea. That's the only reason why I'm even training you. Because you remind me of me when I was younger. The 80's were tough for my community. Which is why I'm here. To help others such as yourself. But it'll be up to you to not let your family down and not waste my time.", he says.

"Yes sir!", I say with excitement.

He tells me and Nia to place our things in his living room for now and tells us to meet him in his front yard in training clothes. Nia says something to me in the living room.

"Hey, sorry for coming off rude earlier.", she tells me.

"Oh…no problem.", I respond.

"It's just that…well I've been training for a long time for this. And I've heard stories how dangerous this tournament is. Literally… anything is legal. And I've heard stories of how dangerous it can get. And with you not having powers, it just worries me that you don't know what you're getting yourself into.", she says.

"I'll be fine, as long as Master Isaiah trains me, I'll complete this and win the tournament.", I say with confidence.

"Woah… calm down with that win word my guy. I'M going to win this, so you can be runner-up if you want."

"Runner-up? I've never been runner-up in my life.", I tell her.

"You've never been a fighter either. So I guess things in life change.", she says.

She walks out the door into the front. I start to think about what she said though. What does she mean anything is legal?

We meet Master Isaiah in the front yard who's waiting for us.

"Bout time you two got out here. If ya'll that slow then don't worry bout entering the tournament.", he tells us both while losing his patients.

I want to ask him more about the tournament but I don't want to seem like I'm worried. I have to toughen up.

"Today we'll start with our 20-mile jog."

"20 miles!? Start?" I say with worry.

"Is that a problem Joseph!? Because it isn't too late for you to go home! Now do you want to win or are you going to keep crying like a punk-ass!", he asks me.

"I want to win sir.", I say like a dog with its tail in between its legs.

"Then shut up and let's get going! Time is precious!" Nia gives me look of sympathy and starts to jog behind Master Isaiah. I follow behind her.

We jog only for a couple of minutes before my ribs start to hurt again. I keep pushing myself so I don't upset Master Isaiah and to show him that I can handle his ways.

"You two only got five months before the tournament begins!", he shouts. "You got a lot of work to do! There are others who have been training years for this! Nia is one of them! We've only done a mile and a half, come on push it!"

Only a mile and a half? My ribs hurt like hell and it feels like I've been running for three hours already. I'm pretty fit. I played sports all my life until I started working. It's this damn rib injury from No Games that's holding me back.

I try and try to push and push, but it becomes too much for me.

"Master…. Isaiah! I….. I can't……. my ribs!", I say trying to catch my breath.

I stop and bend over in pain. He stops and turns around and walks toward me. Then suddenly he punches me as hard as he can right in my ribs. I fall and yell in pain as I lie on the sidewalk.

"I guess I was wrong about you kid! You're just a waste of time!", he tells me.

He turns around. "Try not to die out here kid, also it's a damn shame. You let your mother down. But even worse…… you let your father down….he's disappointed in you. I guarantee it."

I get a look of shock, sadness, and anger all at once. What and how does he know about my dad?

"Don't say nothing bout my dad! Shut up!", I struggle to say pissed off.

"I bet he wanted you to take care of the house and you couldn't even take care of your ribs…just sad. Come on Nia, let's go."

He starts jogging again and although Nia hesitates to leave, she follows behind him.

"Isaiah!!", I shout as I struggle to get to my feet.

"Who the hell you talking to! Nobody talks about my dad!"

It takes me a while to get to my feet, but then off of pure adrenaline and anger, I start to jog again. And over time I get faster, and faster, and faster. I eventually catch up to them again but not close enough to punch Master Isaiah like I want to. I try to get closer to him and I eventually even pass Nia, who's starting to get tired.

As time goes and I keep trying to get close to him, I look around and notice we're back at his house.

"Finished!", he says.

I slow down and Nia stops and catches her breath. I'm too tired to try to fight him so I confront him instead.

"The hell is wrong with you! You don't know nothing about my father old ass man!"

He interrupts me and says, "I know he was shot and killed by a police officer in 2008. I also know you because I saw you and your mother on TV during the riots. I know that it hurt you dearly.", he tells me.

"Ok! Then why the hell you talking about it then!", I ask pissed off.

"You notice you're not talking about your ribs anymore? That pain from your father hurts way more than your ribs do son. And you're alive, able to take care of your family. If you can handle that and survive after the death of your father, then you can handle your ribs.", he explains.

"Yea but that's different. This is physical pain.", I tell him.

"Pain is pain. Nothing physical about it. It's all mental and spiritual. Come inside you two and get some water, we're not done yet."

He goes inside and Nia follows behind. I stand in the front yard and think about what he said. The pain from my ribs do hurt again, but I try to ignore it. I smirk a little bit.

"This is going to be interesting.", I say to myself. I then walk in the house.

While we drink and snack up on food, he tells us to meet him in his basement. We go down the creaking, wooden steps into his basement. He has one dim light that barely lights the room on the ceiling but a bright lamp in the corner. He points to his white bored and tells us this is what we are going to be doing today.

On the bored, it says 500 pushups, 700 sit ups, 800 jump ropes, and a total time of 1 hour of planks. I bite my tongue and don't complain.

"Make sure you don't kill yourself now. Do the pushups in sets no less than 20, same with the sit ups. Do the jump ropes in sets of 100 and hold a plank for at least five minutes. Make sure you have all this done by 5:00pm. I'll be back.", he says.

"Where're you going?", Nia asks.

He looks on his phone and gets a serious look on his face and says sternly, "To take care of business."

Then he exits.

"Welp, there goes our trainer.", I say.

"What's the matter, scared he's not going to be here to hold your hand the whole time?", she says trying to be funny.

"I thought you were going to be nice now.", I say.

"Oh trust me, if you knew me, you would know this is me being nice to you. Plus even though we're training together, doesn't make us allies. You're my competition and I'll beat you in this tournament if need be. Then afterword, maybe we can go out and eat lunch.", she says.

"Um...ok." I don't know if that was a threat or flirt or both. Nia is really pretty but I'm not trying to get my ass kicked trying to be smooth with her. She seems like the ones who hate being hit on. Plus I need to focus on my main goal and that's getting in shape for this tournament. Although with her taking off her jogging suit and being in her sports bra and leggings and seeing how fit she is, it will be hard to focus.

She starts her work outs and so do I, but I do ask her questions about her. If I'm going to be training with her for five months, I might as well get to know her a little bit.

"So Nia... where you from?", I ask.

"ATL. I'm guessing your from here huh?"

"Yeah, homegrown. Well, I'm guessing you're here specifically to train with Master Isaiah."

"So you do know how to connect the dots.", she says with a smirk.

"Yea I'm kind of good at that. If you don't mind me asking, what got you into this tournament?", I ask.

"Well….when your born with powers like this and you have a mom that failed to enter the tournament in the 90s and a money hungry dad, you really don't have a choice. They'll push you to your limits…..just like they did my big sister.", she says. The whole mood changes after that sentence.

"Oh I'm sorry….. you didn't have to tell me all that, I apologize.", I try to explain.

"Oh it's ok, she's not dead or nothing, but they drove her crazy. She started taking drugs and sleeping around and being abused by men. They still blame her to this day and refuse to help her."

"You really don't need to tell me this, I'm sorry.", I say starting to feel bad for asking. I notice small tears coming from her eyes.

"No, it's fine. I heard what Master Isaiah said to you earlier about your dad. If I can come to cope with my pain from my parents, then I feel I can win this thing without anyone hurting me.", she says.

"I guess Master Isaiah is helping more than we thought already huh?", I say trying to lighten up the mood.

"Yea… he really is.", she says as she wipes her tears.

5:00pm hits and me and Nia are not done with our workouts. Almost, but not quite. It's really the planks and pushups that's killing me. But I look over at Nia and is amazed again. She's doing her pushups with her hair.

"How are you doing that?", I ask like a fanboy.

"My power, duh dummy. It's called Hair Control. Every female in my family gets it.", she tells me.

"You must've been training for a long time to get it like that huh?", I ask.

"Yea.", she says smiling.

More time goes by, but Master Isaiah hasn't come back yet. And as 5:30pm hits, he still hasn't showed up.

Me and Nia start to worry.

"You think he got into a fight?", Nia asks.

"I don't know but we are in Memphis so it wouldn't surprise me.", I say.

We hear the front door open and get defensive. Nia gets in a fighting stance that I can tell she's been trained in, while I just put my fist up like a street fighter.

"That's your stance?", she whispers trying not to laugh at me.

"Look leave me alone.", I say.

"Nia! Joseph! Help me with these groceries!" It's Master Isaiah.

We let out a sigh in relief, disbelief, and disappointment all at once. He had a lot of groceries and it hurt a lot carrying them with our sore muscles. After that he asks us were we finished. We wanted to lie but didn't. He said we would finish them later and he tells us to go to the backyard for our last part of training today.

We go back there and finally hear what we've been waiting for.

"It's time, to scrap!", he says.

"Yes!", Nia says in excitement.

"First we'll see what you already know. Nia vs Joseph!", he says like an announcer.

We enter the concrete square surrounded by grass and fighting equipment.

"Scrap!", he yells like an announcer.

I square up but am a little nervous. I've never fought a girl before.

"You better not take it easy on me because I'm a girl! I'll still kick your ass!", Nia says like she was reading my mind. Her tone and vibe has completely changed from calm and nice to a competitive freak. I kind of like it.

"It's kind of hard not to.", I tell her.

I shouldn't have said that cause that seemed to piss her off. She hits me in the face with the two quickest punches I've ever seen and felt in my life.

I swing back but she ducks faster than I did when I fought No Games. She gets low and sweeps me off my feet with her legs.

"Come on Joseph, this all you got? You from Memphis right? You should know how to fight!", she says talking trash. I didn't know Nia was this competitive, but so am I and I won't take this trash talk lightly.

I run at her and swing but she jumps in the air and lands her foot on my face. I fall to the ground hard.

"Oh my!", I hear Master Isaiah saying. "You done?", he asks me.

"No! Not at all!", I struggle to say while spitting out blood. This is tougher than I could ever imagine.

I run at her but this time with her hair she whips me so hard it knocks me on the ground and leaves a bloody whip mark on my face. I try to get up, but my ribs and sore body won't allow me.

"I think this is over.", Nia says.

"Winner Nia! Un-scrapped!", Master Isaiah says.

I'm guessing un-scrapped means she didn't even get touched.

"You got a lot of work to do my friend.", Master Isaiah tells me.

"That's not fair!", I say in anger.

"She has powers! She beat me with her hair!", I say. I regret it instantly because I put myself in this position to fight people with powers. I sound like an idiot, like this wasn't expected. It's part of the territory, but she whooped my ass badly more than I though.

"Sir to be fair, she kicked your ass the whole fight and only used her hair once. Secondly, nothing is going to be fair in this tournament kiddo.", he explains.

It sucks because I know he's right. The only thing I can do is suck up my pride.

"Yes sir.", I say. This fight kind of helps me put things in perspective. What if there are stronger fighters than Nia?

Nia helps me on my feet and is a good sport about it, for now anyways. He tells Nia to go inside and finish her reps. He keeps me outside with him to work on my fighting skills.

"You fight with your emotions, which is good, but you also have to use your brain. You're right, you don't have powers, so you can't rely on your emotions and anger to win a fight.", he explains to me.

"When will I get the power you got? Ze?", I ask ignoring him trying to rush the process and frustratedly.

He then also gets frustrated then grabs me and slams me on the ground. I sit there in pain, regretting the question.

"You're not ready for Ze yet. Not even close. Now get up, I know you're tired of being on the ground like you're looking at the Straight Outta Compton album.", he says.

"You mean the movie?", I ask trying to be funny.

"Oh my God you kids are useless.", he says while face palming himself in disappointment.

"I'm not a kid, I'm 18.", I say.

"Still a kid."

He trains me on my stance and my attacks. He punches, and I practice blocking, and ducking. I'd rather duck than block. Sometimes blocking hurts too. I get hit a few times but return to my feet. I get better as we go. He then shows me how to attack better without being read by an opponent. Again, he reads me a few times, but I get better as we do more reps.

Later that day, we also train on my movements, like flipping away and towards an opponent and dodging. I have some skill in that though, I learned how to do flips in the 6th grade, but he's pushing me to a more extreme level with it. I remember how Nia flipped in the air in the back alley. I have to get like that, or at least close. Nia is very far ahead of me and it kind of sucks just thinking about our skill gap. I'll just have to get better I guess.

The sun goes down and we head back in the house to see Nia practicing her punches and flips. I'm guessing she finished her reps.

"You two done?", she asks.

"Yea.", I say very tiredly.

"Well hopefully tomorrow you'll at least be able to hit me.", she says. I knew the trash talk would come back.

"Oh trust me, I will. I owe you for this scar on my face. I look like Tony Montana.", I say.

"Is that a threat?", she asks.

"No, that's a promise.", I say like a movie character. I swear I did it unintentionally.

They both look in shock and surprise and get a smile on their face.

"OOOOOOOO, look at you!", they both say.

"Mr. my ribs hurt finally sounding like a fighter now.", Nia says and laughs.

"I can tell you've been practicing that line all day in your head, haven't you?", Master Isaiah asks while laughing.

"No. Why are ya'll making this a big deal?", I ask.

I try to hold in my laugh.

Master Isaiah cooks dinner while me and Nia rotate taking cool baths. When I get out I'm greeted by steamy baked chicken, homegrown green beans, biscuits, and mac n cheese. I really don't see dinner like this but try to control myself as I dig in. I feel bad knowing my mom and my sister can't be here for this.

I call them before I go to bed to check in. My mom is doing good for the time being and so is Savannah. I hear Bishop barking in the background and start to tear up. I'm usually not away from my family, at least Savannah and Bishop, and it's weird going a whole day without being home. It's day one and I already miss them. But it pushes me and reminds me that I'm doing this for them…..and my father.

Chapter 4. Normal Teen, Crazy World

I try to sleep, but I'm suddenly awoken by a loud bang noise coming from the backyard. I wake up in confusion, thinking that I'm dreaming, but I hear it again. This time it's so loud it startles me and I fall off the couch.

As I get up trying to remove my blanket, I call for Nia.

"Nia….Nia!", I whisper loudly.

She doesn't respond. I look over to the other couch in the living room and see that she's no longer there. Now I'm starting to get worried.

I hear the loud bang noise again from the backyard. It sounds like an explosion hitting a wall or something.

I creep around the house towards Master Isaiah's room to see if he's there.

"Master Isaiah?", I call out in worry.

As I walk down the hallway, I see his door is wide open, and he's also no longer there. My mind automatically goes to the worst thought or possibility I could think off. What if someone kidnapped them, or killed them? What if No Games and Red Angel wasn't playing and hired someone with powers to get them?

I rush towards the backyard to see what that banging sound is. It has gotten quieter and quieter with each explosion.

To my relief, I see Master Isaiah in the backyard, standing in a pose like he was throwing something at the brick wall surrounding his backyard. I creek the back door open and walk to the edge of his back porch. He's breathing very hard trying to catch his breath, as if he went on another 20-mile jog.

"Did you hear that sound Master Isaiah? And where is Nia?", I ask.

"Yea, that noise was me. Sorry if I woke you up, but I needed to see where my power was. My Ze.", he says.

"Wow, can you show me, like what even is that power?", I ask.

"Nah, not right now. You'll find out yourself, if you're worthy of gaining the power that is.", he tells me.

"Really? Just show me now please!", I beg like a child.

"No need to rush Joseph, if you listen to me you'll be fine. And if you're worried about Nia, don't. I woke her up about an hour and a half ago. She decided to get some exercise in and started to jog around the city again.", he tells me.

"Jogging in Memphis? At night?", I say concerningly.

"Yea. Is that a problem?", he asks.

"Yea, this place is crazy! You're kind of old so I know you've heard the song or phrase the freaks come out at night. And she's a girl, she could get kidnapped or something.", I say sounding like my mom.

"Nia is strong, she'll be alright. And stop the girl crap now. Don't forget she beat you up pretty badly not too long ago. You sound like you like her or something and you've only just met her.", he says.

"WHAT! No! I just see it like if my little sister Savannah went jogging at night in Memphis. It's too dangerous.", I tell him as my black face turns red as much as it possibly can.

"If you're so concerned, go get her then Joseph.", he says sounding very annoyed.

"Fine.", I say. I walk back into the house and put my shoes on. I keep my black tank top on and my red shorts.

I walk out the front door and begin to walk. I take the same path we took earlier today while we were jogging.

I begin to jog but the longer I go, the more worried I get and I slow down. I don't get worried for me, but I do for Nia. And the fact that she's not from around here bothers me even more. I know she has powers, but if she gets jumped by people with powers, or shot, it'll be a terrible situation.

I walk for a little bit longer. I end up in downtown Memphis. I see some drug heads and other night life people staring at me suspiciously. I keep on walking and I try to ignore them. If I make it back to Master Isaiah's house before I find Nia, sadly, I'm going to have to call the cops, and I really, REALLY, don't want to have to call them.

I walk almost all the way down the street, but as soon as I begin to turn on the other street, I hear a man call out to me.

"Aye boy!", I hear an old voice call out. I ignore it and keep on walking.

"Aye kid, you looking for someone?", he calls out again.

I keep on walking, trying even harder to ignore him.

"You looking for that girl right? That black girl with the long hair?", he asked.

I finally stopped and turned around. I know that he's talking exactly about Nia.

"Yeah, I am. You seen her around here?", I ask in a tough voice. You have to be tough around here.

"Yeah. She came down here jogging. I heard her screaming a few streets down though.", he says.

"Where!?", I ask very concerningly.

"HERE!"

I hear a loud voice right behind me. It's so loud I jump a little bit as it startles me. As soon as it says here, I feel something big wrap around my leg and lift me from the ground upside down like Nia did. But it keeps lifting me up way higher than Nia did.

As I rise up, I see a man with a tentacle, octopus like lower half body. He stands at least 25 feet tall. He must be using his powers of course.

"Let me go!!!", I scream.

"You're coming with me kiddo!", he tells me.

He then runs, or crawls, or whatever down a back alley between two buildings with me stuck in his grasp. The old man must have set me up.

"The little girl got away from me, but you're a way easier prey! You won't put up nearly as a good fight as her!", he tells me.

"You tryna eat me weirdo!!? Do octopuses even eat meat!!?", I asked very worriedly.

"Duh idiot! Pay attention in class and you would've known that!", he tells me.

He finally stops in a dark area. He lifts me eye level to him and I get a good look at him. I can't believe my eyes.

"Mr. Ashland!!!?", I say very surprised. The monster trying to eat me, is my 12th grade homeroom teacher.

"Yes Joseph! I finally let lose! I couldn't hold the urge to not use my powers anymore. How the hell is using my powers a sin when I've been blessed with them!? To hell with that! To hell with society! If it's a sin and under the sin of Kronos, than fine! I don't care if I sin! I want to use it!", he rants.

" I don't care but why me though!?", I ask.

"Sorry Joseph, you just so happen to come across my path. But you should be honored. You're the first victim but the first part of this revolution!", he preaches.

"What revolution!?", I ask trying to free myself.

"The revolution of true freedom. I've been awoken by the words of Free Power and I'm ready to truly be free! And I'm very hungry Joseph!", he tells me.

"Then eat a burger or something weirdo!"

"Sorry but the animal in me won't settle for baby food much longer!", he shouts.

"OCTOPUSES DON'T EAT PEOPLE!", I yell getting scared and angry.

"SHUT UP JOSEPH AND LET IT HAPPEN!", he shouts back.

This man has certainly lost it, but it may cost me my life.

Right as he's about to eat me, which is weird to even say, someone interrupts.

"HEY!!"

I know that voice, and I'm glad to hear it. It's Nia.

"You again, why are you here!?", Mr. Ashland asks in frustration.

"I should be asking you the same question you weirdo. Now how many times do I have to teach you this lesson old man? I've already whooped your ass earlier today, I guess I have to do it again.", she says.

"You escaped me last time, but this time I'll eat you and him!", he yells.

"We'll see about that!", she says.

Mr. Ashland slams a tentacle at Nia, but she dodges it and rolls out the way. She tries to grab it, but he flicks her off of his tentacle and tosses her. She hits a building.

"Nia!", I yell as she lies on the ground unconscious.

"You thought I'd fall for the same trick twice!", he says then starts to laugh.

She tries to struggle to her feet, but he grabs her too. I know I have to help her some way, but I don't know how. I then instantly bite his tentacle that's wrapped around my body. He lets out a scream in pain and drops me and Nia. Nia falls hard, still unable to get on her feet.

"Nia…", I start to say. But he swipes his tentacle hard at me. I go flying into a metal dumpster.

"I'm supposed to eat you not the other way around you idiot! No wonder why you're failing!", he says in anger.

Nia starts to get back on her feet.

"This ends now!", he yells.

"SHUT UP! I'M TRYING TO GET SOME SLEEP! I GOT WORK IN THREE HOURS YOU IDIOT!!!", some man in one of the buildings says to Mr. Ashland.

"Sorry but this is way more important than your stupid minimum wage job punk.", Mr. Ashland response back.

"Didn't you say you were a teacher fool! Yea, like you make a big check yourself!", another woman says from another window.

"You watch yourself before I eat you too!", Mr. Ashland says loudly.

"Mane, eat these nuts!", another man says.

"HOW DARE YOU!", Mr. Ashland says in disgust.

As he argues with the other people. I see Nia get up to her feet. She looks at me and signals me to stay quiet as she sneaks around Mr. Ashland. As she exits my sight and gets behind Mr. Ashland, they stop arguing.

"Damn it, where's that girl now?", Mr. Ashland says.

"HERE!", Nia yells.

She leaps high into the air and wraps her hair around his neck. He struggles to get her off of him. It's like she's riding a wild bull, trying to hold on with dear life. He eventually gives up as Nia's grip gets tighter and tighter. His bottom half of his body turns back into normal and he falls to the ground unconsciously. Only problem is, he's naked from the bottom down now.

"That's gross!", Nia says.

"Yeah it is, but are you ok?", I ask.

'I'm good. Are you ok? How many times do I have to save you though?", she asks jokingly.

"I came out here to look for you!", I respond in frustration.

"Yea, well bout time you left, I was already back at the house. He told me you were gone and the first thing that hit my head was "He's gonna run into the octopus man." And it seems I was right.", she says. She smiles and gives me a playful punch to the arm.

We then here police sirens.

"Shoot! We gotta go!", I say.

"Yea agreed!", she response back.

We both dash through the other alley and leave before the cops arrive. We jog all the way back to Master Isaiah's house. He greets us both at the door.

"Well…how did it go?", he asks.

We both just nod our heads very tiredly. And then we both rush to the couches and pass out. Before I fade away to sleep, I hear Master Isaiah say, "These two may make it after all."

Chapter 5. Faith

The next few weeks goes very similar, except the whole killer teacher thing. It's a little harder to keep up with the jogs without me being angry at Master Isaiah, but me knowing I've done it before pushes me to keep going. I keep up with my reps as we continue as well and overtime I even notice that I'm getting bigger, faster, and stronger, but Nia and Master Isaiah always humbles me whenever my head gets too big.

Speaking of Nia, weeks go by and while I do get better, I still don't even touch her in our combat trainings. Every time I get close to hitting her she just uses her hair. Every day after training it pisses me off so much that I didn't touch her and that she's beating me without even trying.

And for some reason, Master Isaiah has been making a real big emphasis on meditation, and my faith in God. Why? I have no clue but it's pissing me off and he wastes a lot of time, that could be dedicated to fighting, on dumb stuff like meditating.

I ask him does this play a role in me getting Ze a lot but every time I bring up Ze he just punches me and tells me to worry about my faith instead.

These past few days I've been very pissed and angry. I'm not improving in my fights despite my hard work, and I've been meditating for hours every day and still have no powers. One night while eating dinner with Master Isaiah I snap.

"I'm wasting my time!", I say out loud. "How am I not getting better!?"

"What are you talking about?", Master Isaiah asks in confusion.

"I've been busting my ass off every day and still can't even touch her! And she's not even using her powers! And it's been weeks on top of weeks and I still don't have Ze! I kept my end of the deal! You said if I work hard, you'll get me ready, and I have but I haven't gotten any better!", I yell in frustration while slamming my fist into the table.

He gets up and punches me in the chest so hard I fall to the ground.

"One, don't ever yell at me. And two, I said I would push you past your physical and mental limits. It's up to you to use them to your advantage. And if you quit being so damn worried on Ze and focus on faith, you'll be closer than you are now! Ze doesn't just come to anyone seeking power! It comes to those who believe in their hearts, not their heads!", he says.

"Believe in what!?", I ask in anger trying to catch my breath.

"God and the goodness in Earth idiot!", he says.

"How can I believe in God when I grew up in hell huh!? If there was a God, then why would he put me in hell my whole life instead of heaven huh? I would be in a big house with my mom and dad. Without living in a neighborhood where people die every day! That's what God does! But I guess I'm not good enough for that huh? Or Ze!", I say in anger trying to hold back tears.

I seem to catch him off guard. He pauses and tries to catch himself.

"Life is hell kid. It's a test to see who's worthy of heaven. It's up to you to make it, but only YOU can decide that. Not me, Nia, or your family! You have to actually feel it in your heart Joseph!", he explains

"That's what Ze is Joseph, it's faith. Even if you don't want to believe in God you MUST find the POSITIVE in life! You must gain a positive spirit inside you Joseph.", he says looking down at me, like he sees someone else in me.

The whole house goes silent and all we can hear is Nia's music as she takes her bath.

He goes back to his chair as I rise back up and take a seat shamefully.

"Plus, if you must know you have gotten better. You've been here for a little over a month and I haven't heard you complain about your ribs since the first day. You've been keeping up with our jogs and your workouts. This takes time and I've been training you as fast as I can. Nia has been doing this her whole life. Don't think you're on her level yet.", he says.

"Yes sir.", I say.

Nia walks out the bathroom and jumps to the table for food.

"What was all the commotion about?", she asks.

"Nothing.", Master Isaiah says. "Now for the real announcement. Next month there will be an exhibition event for those looking to enter the tournament."

"Really!?", Nia says in excitement.

"Yes really. Now if I didn't think you were ready, I wouldn't have signed you up.", he says.

"You mean ya'll?", I say to him.

"No. I meant right. I signed you up Nia. Joseph, you'll have to prove to me for the rest of this month you can handle this tournament."

Nia gets happy and excited, as she should, and I want to show her how happy I am for her, but I can't. With anger I say yes sir and get up from the table without finishing my food and go to lay down in the living room.

It's kind of awkward because they can still see me in the living room from the kitchen. I usually call my mom and check on them every day, but I'm too mad to do that.

"Is he ok?", I hear Nia whispering.

"He'll be fine.", Master Isaiah whispers back.

The next day I make sure to go even harder than before at everything. I keep up with Master Isaiah in my jogging the whole time. He's boosted us up to 40 miles with breaks now but I still manage to stay with him. I go hard on my reps as well. I still don't even touch Nia that day though, but I don't give up hope. Whenever I have something to prove to someone, I'll prove it. And I must do that to make the exhibition.

Another week goes by without me touching Nia, but after our fights I take in and soak every detail Master Isaiah shows and tells me after me and Nia's fights. My stance and overall fighting have gotten better but not good enough. I fully relax my mind during my meditation segments. I try talking to God more and coming to terms with my life, and how it's up to me to change it.

I've never been too religious of a person, but I try to fully understand and believe within myself. Even though I've had it tough, I'm still alive with a family. I try to find the peace and blessings I guess I have.

But one particular day, me and Nia are going at it again. She has also gotten better overtime. Master Isaiah trains her one on one on her fighting too after me and him are done. I watch them though because their training is way more intense then mines.

But today me and Nia are fighting and over the time being, I've notice how she fights. She usually lets me charge in and then she attacks based off me. So this time I relax a little, not a lot though to let her know I'm still alert.

"What's the matter? Scared to swing today?", she asks me.

I stay silent and focused. I keep my distance because her hair can grab me at any moment, but that's when it hits me. I get back and try to bait her to use her hair. It works and she whips it to me and I grab it, pulling her to me and then I knee her right in her stomach. She falls to the ground in shock. Master Isaiah is shocked as well.

She smiles and gets up and tells me good job. But then she drops back on the ground and tries to sweep me off my feet, but I jump over her legs. Once she misses, she tries to whip me with her hair but I jump, run, dodge them. She runs up to me quickly though and lands a nice kick in my stomach. As I bend over in pain she hits me with a scissor kick knocking me to the ground.

I can't get up after that and blood is leaking slowly from my forehead.

"Oh I'm sorry!", she says. Master Isaiah doesn't call the match.

She helps me up but as she does I grab her and toss her, backwards back first to the ground. She lies there in pain and gets mad.

"I was trying to help you asshole!", she yells.

"Nia, you know good and well that if I don't call the match, then it's not over!", Master Isaiah tells her.

She gets up and charges in anger with multiple hair attacks while yelling. I know I have her where I want her. I get hit a few times, but she's trying to hit me with all heavy attacks. Master Isaiah taught us that in fighting, there are light attacks, medium attacks, and heavy attacks, just like a video game. If someone misses a heavy attack, it's easier to punish them.

I do just that and dodge another heavy hair attack and kick her directly in her stomach, knocking her back the ground. It was a strong kick and she doesn't get up.

"Match! Joseph wins!", Master Isaiah says. I had finally won.

She gets up and despite the heated match, she shakes my hand and congratulates me.

"Now I'm going to have to really start trying on you soon.", she says.

"Sure." I say sarcastically.

"While that was impressive, you still have more work to do before I qualify you for the exhibition.", Master Isaiah tells me.

"What? But I won.", I say in shock and in sadness.

"Yea and she's beat you over 50 times.", he says.

"I only have one more week to register Master. If I don't get in to make a name for myself then I'll stand no chance. What will I do?", I ask in hopelessness.

"That's for you to find out.", he says. Then he walks inside and Nia follows behind.

I sit on a chair that's outside and I sit there for a while as the sun sets. I get angry and throw the chair against the brick wall. Then I sit in the concrete match square and cry.

"I'm letting everyone down. What can I do?", I ask myself in tears.

The sky gets darker and I still sit on the ground. I hear the door creak open and look behind me to see Nia.

She comes and takes a seat next to me.

"You know, you never came in to heal your forehead?", she says.

She hands over a big band-aid for me to put over my cut.

"Nia, how do you keep going, even when it seems like everything and everyone is against you and the pressure is all on you?", I ask.

"What you mean?", she asks.

"I have to look out for my family Nia. My mom is getting sicker, I quit school for this but that doesn't matter because I wasn't going to college anyways. And here I am….not even able to qualify for an exhibition. I don't know, maybe this was a waste of time."

"Maybe it was.", she says. I look at her with a face of disappointment.

"But maybe it wasn't. That's up for you to decide. But I know why I keep going. It's to help my sister and to prove something to my parents.", she says.

"And that is….?", I ask.

"That I can do this without them. Why do you think I'm here? I told them I could do it without their help and that I'll do this not for them but for me and my sister. As soon as I turned 18 I flew out here for Master Isaiah."

"Wow….. you really were determined huh?", I say.

"I still am. I keep my faith in God and the angels above, and do it for me and my sister, and with that, I'm all set to do anything I want." She stands up.

"Your time will come too Joseph. I can tell you care about your family too. You won't let them down, I promise.", she says.

"Thanks Nia.", I say. She smiles and walks back in the house.

I get up and get in my trained fighting stance. I close my eyes and take a deep breath and I practice my punches and attacks with my eyes close. I mix my training from Master Isaiah and my meditation segments into one.

As I keep going, I get more and more intense with it. "Faith.", I say to myself over and over again. I keep going for at least 30 minutes.

"Faith."

"Faith."

"Faith."

"I'll say it over and over again, until I'm sure I'll win."

I try to think how lucky, or blessed I am to even be alive after all I've been through and where I live and come from. Although my dad is dead, he still watches over me. I still have my mom, Savannah, and Bishop. I have Jamal, Jax, and all the other people in my city who actually care. I know I can get it. Master Isaiah obviously saw something in me. That's why he allowed a random 18-year-old to train with him. I just have to believe in myself now.

I then open my eyes finally to see that my hands are glowing white.

"WOAH!!!", I say out loud.

It scares me at first and I jump, but then I realize what it was.

"ZE!!!", I say out loud.

"SHUT UP I'M TRYNA SLEEP IDIOT! I'VE BEEN HEARING YOU YELL FAITH FOREVER NOW! BE QUIET!", I hear a neighbor in the house behind us say.

"Sorry!", I say timidly.

The white glow fades away slowly though and I get upset.

"No….NO! Come back! Damn it!"

I rush into the house and dash to Master Isaiah's door banging it. Nia wakes up in the living room in anger.

"Master Isaiah!!! Wake up! I did it!", I say like a little kid.

"Did what? And why are you so loud? It's 11:00pm!", Nia says.

I keep banging and Master Isaiah finally opens the door and with an open hand, he just bops me in the face and I fall back against the wall hard.

"The hell is wrong with you kid?! All on my door this late!", he says while rubbing his eyes.

I didn't even notice how long I was outside. I thought I only trained for 30 minutes. I guess I was out longer than I thought.

"I did it! I had Ze!", I say in excitement.

"What? Boy go back to sleep.", he says dismissing my claim.

"No seriously! My hands were glowing white!"

He pauses. "What? Are you sure?", he asks.

"I saw it with my own eyes!", I say.

"But how…..?", he says looking very lost and puzzled.

"Is everything ok Master?", Nia asks.

"Nobody ever has gotten Ze that fast naturally….ever. It's impossible…..but you named the right color of it.", he says while talking to himself.

Nia looks at me and smiles. "Told you.", she says.

"Well then…Joseph, consider yourself qualified for the tournament next week.", he tells me.

"Yes!!!", I say happily.

"But don't think we're done yet. We're not even close. You still need to go hard, you hear me?", he asks me.

"Yessir. ", I say with energy.

For once, I go to sleep happy. As I cover up, Nia gives me thumbs up.

"Thank you.", I say.

"No problem.", she response on the other couch.

The next day starts off very good. I know it's going to be special, because Master Isaiah skips everything and says we'll be fighting all day. We go straight to the backyard.

"Now Joseph, you finally have proven to be worthy of Ze, but now you must know how to use it and not abuse it. Nia, Joseph, I want you two to fight. But now, go all out. Use all you got, mental power, physical power, but still with your emotion.", he tells us both.

We both nod and get in the square and shake hands.

"Now Scrap!", Master Isaiah says.

Me and Nia start our fight very intensely. Trading blows, dodging attacks, and reading each other. I'm physically stronger, but with her still able to use her hair and being quicker than me, she still has a huge advantage. She still is an overall better fighter.

I don't know how to use my Ze but I need to learn quickly in order to win. I'm starting to slip and get sloppy in my fighting, and she notices. She then wraps her hair around my neck to put me to sleep.

"Give up!", she yells desperately.

"No!", I struggle to say back.

I try to get my hand to her face to grab her but fail. But as I reach, my hands start getting that white glow around it again. This time though, it's also surrounded by white smoke

"Wow…", I hear Master Isaiah say quietly but amazed.

Then suddenly, a big white, smoky like ball forms from my hands. It gets bigger and hotter in my hand as I hold it. I feel my arm getting tighter and tighter like I'm holding something heavy. I loosen my arm and the Ze blast releases towards Nia. She dodges it, but at least I'm not being choked anymore.

"Nice one.", she says in amazement with her eyes wide open.

"Nice one indeed my friend.", we hear an unfamiliar voice say.

We look up to see a Japanese man standing on the back porch. He has on a robe that says 91' TTS Winner, and a Japanese flag on it. He's about 6'3, the same height as Master Isaiah. Although I've never met this man in my life, I can still feel some tense history in the air, and now I feel me and Nia are now part of it.

"Jiro!", Master Isaiah says in shock. He must know this guy.

"Master Jiro, to you my friend Isaiah.", Jiro says.

"You're not my friend, and you have no business here! Now leave!"

I've never seen Master Isaiah get this defensive. Almost as if he was being threatened.

"Calm my friend, I bring no harm, just checking up on the next fighters. You know, I thought you would throw this life away after I had beaten you."

"That has nothing to do with now Jiro.", Master Isaiah says.

"But it does! Your country turned their backs on you, while mines embraced me. Left you homeless and almost dead, didn't I. I told you that you're wasting your time trying to train new fighters.", Jiro says.

"You had NOTHING to do with that! My country already hated me! Because I didn't stand for them and what they were doing to my people! You were just the cover up they needed. You think I don't know the truth Jiro?", Master Isaiah says in anger.

A pause happens as Master Isaiah stares at Jiro and he stares back.

"You weren't worthy of Ze and you know it! They taught you and gave it to you and you used it till you could master it!", Master Isaiah says.

"But I did it better my friend. Trained and became better than you! Just like Haru will!"

"Who's that!?", I interject.

"Joseph! Stay out of this." , Nia tells me.

"No, I'm not going to let anyone disrespect my master.", I tell her.

"Oh boy, you just don't understand.", Jiro says to me.

He then looks back at Master Isaiah but he continues talking to me.

"Haru is a level 65 Ze user! And from what I witness just now, you're just now tapping into level 1."

He then looks back at me.

"In other words, you stand no chance, just like your master did."

"We can settle this right here, right now Jiro.", Master Isaiah says in his normal but stern voice. Jiro laughs and chuckles. It's one of those, I'm better than you chuckles.

"I have nothing to prove to you anymore…..my friend."

Master Isaiah charges up a big bright Ze ball and throws it at Jiro, but he dodges it and throws one back. Master Isaiah barely dodges it but it explodes causing him to fall and destroying some of the backyard.

"Master!", Nia says in a panic. Me and her get in our stance to fight, but Jiro just laughs at us.

"You two couldn't beat me if your life depended on it." He then turns around and walks away. He says one more thing before he leaves though.

"Hope to see you at the exhibition next week."

We help Master Isaiah to his feet. We try to deescalate the problematic scene. Using your powers is illegal for citizens and if anyone finds out or tells the cops it can be a big problem.

As we help Master Isaiah into the house, Nia asks him something.

"Master with all due respect, I think now is time you tell us everything. Who was he, what is Ze, and what really happened in the 1991 tournament?"

"Nothing!", he snaps.

He jumps up from the couch and walks to his room.

"Just be ready next week!", he says as he slams his door.

"Seems like we really got to win now, we're fighting for him now too. But level 65 Ze user? What does that even mean?", Nia asks.

"I don't know, but I got faith so I'll win. Even for Master Isaiah."

Chapter 6. The Origin of Ze

Later that day, me and Nia keep on training with each other. About 6 hours in, Master Isaiah comes out the house into the backyard. We both pause as he walks to us. He seems a little bit calmer, but I can tell he's still bothered from earlier.

"It's about time I tell you both the full story now.", he says after a deep breath.

We both take a seat on the concrete.

"As you both know I won the first tournament in 1987. But when I came back, I was met with hostility. It was only $500,000 then, but I used all of my money to help my family, community, and all black ghettos around America. America wanted me to, I guess, show equal love. And for the next tournament they wanted me to represent with an American outfit, hence why we have a Mr. USA fighter every year now. I declined due to the mistreatment of my people. It was the 80's so you have to remember crack and police abuse was at a boiling point. Once I declined, I was blackballed. It seems everyone hated me and to make sure I wouldn't win again, they stole Ze."

"How did they do that?", I asked.

"Ze is a lesser energy form that originated from a power called Zen. You may not have heard of that power before. It's not as common as speed or strength. In fact, the last recorded person with it was a guy named Kaine in the 60's. He almost destroyed the world, hence the reason why we as citizens, are not allowed to use powers at all unless granted permission. Zen is a special power that comes from ancient Africa. With that knowledge, America did what it always does to Africa, steal. They forced the people over there with Ze to teach them the power. To try and hide the fact that they did so, they gave it to Japan's best upcoming fighter, Jiro."

"Wait, wait, what's the difference between Zen and Ze?", Nia asks.

"And why Jiro?", I ask.

"Zen is the original power that people were born with a long time ago. It's way, way stronger than Ze. Ze is more of a technique that people can truly gain from faith and pureness that stems from Zen. And they really didn't care who won the tournament, as long as it wasn't me. Jiro was already an up-and-coming martial artist, so they gave it to him."

"Gave?", Nia asks.

"Yea. He didn't earn it. Ze can be passed down as well. Once America forced the African leaders to teach them the power, they passed it to Jiro."

"So how did he beat you? If you both had Ze?", I ask.

"That.....I honestly don't know. He overpowered me with ease. His Ze was somehow way stronger than mines, which led many people, including me, to believe he was using a power enhancer called Khaos. But that theory got shut down by everyone because they thought I was just being a sore loser, so I let it go. I found out Jiro was here the first day I trained you both."

"That's when you left for a long time?", I ask.

"Yea. He's here for the exhibition America is hosting. He has two trainees, Akio, and Haru. Apparently he's a level 65 Ze user.", he says with concern.

"Is that good?", I ask.

"At my max, I was only level 50."

"Damn.", Nia says.

"That's a problem.", I say.

"That doesn't matter! He's only intimidation so don't worry about the numbers! You must keep faith, and give it your all, both of you! Got it!?", he says as his energy level rises. I can see the white smoke around him now.

"Yessir!", we both say.

"Now Nia, you should work on your speed for your attacks. It's very good but could be better. Joseph! You work on your attacks as well but mainly your Ze."

We both get to work and train for the rest of the day. We don't focus on fighting to win, we instead spar, trying to improve the other. As the sun sets, Master Isaiah cook us another fat meal. We eat, and go to sleep, excited for the upcoming exhibition.

Chapter 7. Nia at The Exhibition

The day is finally here for the exhibition. We eat a good breakfast and pack our bags. I call my mom and sister before I leave and then we head to California for the event. It's being hosted by the Time to Scrap team and we'll be placed in a hotel for a weekend. This is to see who's likely to win the official tournament, analyst to watch and report and to rank people, and for some people to realize they aren't ready. I won't let that be me.

A few hours later we arrive to California and drive to the event. The hotel was made specially for this so it has multiple training rooms, restaurants, and most importantly a giant room that was designed for multiple fights to be held at once. As we tour the place, me and Nia are distracted and amazed by our environment.

"They went all out with this.", Nia says.

"Yea they did. You nervous?", I ask her.

"I mean a little, but once I'm in a match it'll go away quickly.", she responds.

"How do you know?", I ask her.

"Because I don't want to lose."

"Guess that makes sense.", I say.

"Remember, you two have what it takes, just make sure you have faith and don't let anyone intimidate you. If they do then you've already lost. If you need comfort, remember, you were trained by the G.O.A.T.", Master Isaiah assures us.

We put our things in our room and walk to the event room. Some people are warming up with each other but the room is crowded with people. There's at least 200 people and me and Nia are overwhelmed. Then a man on the stage calls everyone to him.

"Everyone, everyone! We know you're all excited for the exhibition but hold your horses! Now take a look on the monitor behind me and go to your designated fighting ring!"

The giant monitor lowers from the ceiling and it shows everyone and who they're fighting and where.

Someone speaks out in disgusts amongst the crowd of people.

"Is this a joke!? How dare I be put in a match with a female! This is a waste of my time!"

He's a tall, Hispanic man who seems to live in the gym. He's long and slinky but built at the same time. He hides his hands in his green boxing shorts with no shirt or shoes on, but with tattoos covering his body.

"Look at this asshole?", Nia whispers to me.

"I'll be better off fighting a child, they might actually stand a chance!", he continues.

Some laugh at his joke.

"I got to stand up to this punk.", Nia tells me getting more irate.

"Nia no, stay out of it.", I try to tell her.

She ignores me and speaks up.

"Sounds like you're scared to me! What's wrong, can't handle a woman!?", Nia says to the guy.

Some look in awe and in shock.

"Woman please.", he says as some others continue to laugh.

"Woman?", Nia says. "I have a name! You call me Nia! Got it punk!"

"Oh so you're the one they put me against. Look if you shut up and learn your place like a woman should, maybe I'll take it easy on you."

"Hey that's enough!", I say.

"No Joseph, I can handle this.", she tells me then redirects her attention to the man.

"You're only like 5'6, you couldn't beat me even if Kronos himself blessed you with all the powers in the world."

"Sounds like you're a woman hater.", Nia responds.

She looks at the monitor to see his name that's matched up against her. It's Killer Carlos.

"What's the matter Carlos? You sound hurt, like a woman did something to you in the past. Well what was it? Broke up with you? Beat your ass? Did your momma leave you as a baby Carlos?"

The crowd feeds into the trash talk and the room fills with "OOOOOOOO's" from everyone. Carlos's face is filled with anger.

"You leave my mother out of this!", he says with anger.

"Oh I know, maybe a woman said you couldn't hang with her in the bed with your TINY problem you got between your legs? Which is it Carlos?"

The crowd now starts to laugh at Carlos. I guess Nia was right when she said she was being nice to me.

"Meet me in the ring then punk girl!", Carlos says.

"Bet!", Nia response with a high competitive energy.

They go to their match area and some people follow behind to finish watching the drama.

"I'll follow her, you find your opponent.", Master Isaiah tells me.

"Ok.", I respond.

 He follows her and I continue to search for my name. When I do find it, my heart stops and my soul leaves my body.

"WAIT WHAT!!!!", I say loudly. "My first match is against Mr. USA!? This is just an exhibition, why is he here!?", I say in fear.

Some guy that looks like he works for the tournament puts his hands on my shoulders.

"He never gives up a chance at fighting son. Goodluck. You're going to need it.", he says.

I'm going to need time to prosses this. My first match is against the winner of the last tournament. It's not until a few hours though so I walk over to Nia's match to try to clear my mind.

People are surrounding them watching. The announcer calls out both of them and their powers.

"From Atlanta Georgia, at 5'6 weighing 135 pounds and 18 years of age, Nia! Power, Hair Control!"

Many people cheer for her, especially women, and chant Nia.

"And from Mexico City Mexico, at 6'9 weighing 240 pounds and 23 years of age, Killer Carlos! Power, Metal Bones!"

A mixture of cheers and boos for him.

He chuckles and then reveal his hands that he's been hiding from us. All of his flesh is gone on his hands, exposing his metal bones.

"His hits are going to hurt like hell Nia! Get in his head and read him!", Master Isaiah tells her.

"Yessir!", she responds.

"Scrap!", the announcer yells.

A lot of other matches are going on right now, but people have their focus on Nia and Killer Carlos. Killer Carlos charges right at her and swings a hard right, but Nia ducks under and ends up behind him. Before he turns around, she uses her hair and wraps it around his neck and slams him to the ground hard back first. People cheer.

"Is that all you got?", she says to him. He gets up chuckling.

"You're dead!", he yells.

He then throws a series of powerful punches and jabs. Nia is very quick and does a good job at dodging them. She punches him a few times, but he blocks and dodges as well. I'm sure it's hard for him to take damage due to his metal bones though. He's definitely a boxer with the way he's fighting.

He charges and swings again but this time when Nia dodges and ends up behind him, and he swings a nasty elbow to her back, sending her down in pain. She screams in pain.

"Ah, the metal elbow, it never fails!", he says then laughs loudly.

"Come on Nia! Get up!", I say.

"Yea listen to your guy, get up bitch!", Killer Carlos mocks.

He kicks her all the way across the room. As she flies across the room, people cringe and squeal as if they've been kicked too. She hits the wall hard. She lies on the ground unresponsive.

"You didn't have to do all of that you sissy! Pick on someone your on size!", I yell as I start to get pissed. I try to run up on him, but Master Isaiah holds me back.

"It's part of the tournament Joseph! Calm down she'll be fine!", Master Isaiah says.

"Forget that! Come kick me like that clown!", I continue to yell as I get more and more pissed off. People stare at me in shock.

"Please, you're not my size either punk. You might as well be a girl! Now what did I say, women are nothing to me!", he says.

"Come on Nia! Remember your sister! Get up!", Master Isaiah yells across the room. Everyone pauses and watches intensely. My body starts to smoke up fully. I notice the white smoke around my body, but I pay it no attention as all of my focus is directed towards Killer Carlos.

People look at me and some awe out loud. Master Isaiah is even taken by surprise.

"JOSEPH! Calm down now!", he yells at me.

I stop trying to go at Killer Carlos and the smoke disappears.

"Interesting power you got there kid. What is it?", Killer Carlos asks with a dirty grin on his face. I don't say anything and I just flick him off.

Right as the announcer is about to call the match, Nia stumbles to her feet and people cheer as she walks back to their fighting square.

"Oh back for more huh? You were talking about my problem in my legs and you can't even handle me.", Killer Carlos says.

"You called me a bitch.", Nia says. "That's when you lost." Her voice sounds like Master Isaiah when he's serious, not loud, but very stern.

She then runs up to him then jumps and spins her body and turns around very fast. She spins so fast that you can't even really see her, only a blur, and all four of her long braids are spread out, spinning like a helicopter. I know from experience that her hair hits hard as hell, but at this speed, it could kill someone.

Killer Carlos tries to catch her without having enough time to react but ends up getting hit with the attack instead. You can hear her hair clanking off of his metal bones. He ends up on the ground, bloody, and in pain. Me and Master Isaiah watch in shock as everyone else cheers her on. Carlos tries to get up but as he does Nia doesn't let up and wraps her hair around his neck until he taps.

"Winner, Nia!", the announcer calls.

People cheer her on and she comes to me and Master Isaiah.

"What, was that?!", I ask in shock. "I've never seen that one before!"

"I don't tell you all of my secrets Joseph.", she says and smiles.

"Good job Nia. I didn't want to tell you this because I didn't want the pressure to hit you but, this is really to see who qualifies for the tournament and all you had to do was win one match to be qualified.", Master Isaiah says.

"Really!?", she says in excitement.

"Yep, you get three chances to win. Today, tomorrow and Sunday. You won the first day so for the rest of your time here, enjoy your vacation."

"YESSS!" She hugs Master Isaiah.

"I wish you would have waited to say that.", I say nervously.

"Oh you'll win too Joseph, it's easy.", Nia says.

"Who do you fight first?", Master Isaiah asks.

"Mr. USA.", I say in a depressed tone.

"Oh...", Master Isaiah says.

"Joseph…..", Nia starts.

"No it's fine, I'll have more chances. You two go celebrate, I'll join you two later.", I say and walk away.

"Joseph!", Nia yells, but I walk off. I think Master Isaiah held her back.

THE AMERICAN HERO VS. THE KID FORM THE HOOD!!!

Chapter 8. Joseph VS Mr. USA!

The time comes around. I go to my area before anyone else and wait. I start to remember why I'm here and get a little confidence, but then I feel a huge hand on my shoulder.

"Yo why does everyone here keep touching……me……", I say.

As I turn around I see a giant white man behind me with a big detective hat in an all red, white, and blue outfit under a coat.

"Are you Joseph?", he asks in a country voice.

"Um……yea…..", I say. "I'm guessing your Mr. USA."

"SHHHHHHH!", he says as he spits all on me. "I don't want everyone over here noticing me, not yet anyways. Look, you can't beat me alright, so let's have a quick, quiet match ok."

"Look mane, even if I did agree to that, they gonna hear a loud ass announcer call our match and your name. And when you take that coat off they gonna see yo big ass in that American suit.", I try explain to him while getting slightly irritated.

He grabs an announcer with one hand and brings him to me fast. The announcer is scared.

"I'm not going to take my coat off, and he's going to call the match, quietly." He looks at the announcer. "Isn't that right?", he threatens.

"Yesss……yessir! Wait…..are you Mr. USA!?", the announcer says loud enough to gather attention.

"Mr. USA?", people start saying.

"Damn it, welp I tried.", he says. He takes off his hat and coat and shows himself to everyone.

"Yes, it is I, Mr. USA! The true real American hero!"

People gather around him and cheer. Some even ask for autographs, even fighters.

"Now watch as I destroy Joseph in under 30 seconds!"

"What?", I say with my voice cracking. All my confidence that I somehow managed to gather is now instantly gone.

We ready up in the ring. My outfit is kind of lame. I wear a black, tank top with a white stripe going down the side to represent the white Ze. The pattern continues with my shorts with the stripe. I wear a white ninja headband and black and white Jordan 5s. Mr. USA is wearing a bright red, white, and blue body suit dressed like a superhero with muscles I've never seen before on someone.

I see Master Isaiah and Nia show up and support.

"Let's go Joseph!", Nia chants.

"From Memphis Tennessee, standing at 6'0 and 174 pounds at 18 years of age, Joseph! Power, unknown." I hear Nia cheering for me and maybe ten others but that's it. I wish I was as cool as her. She had a crowd of people cheering for her.

"And from Dallas Texas, at 6'8 weighing 380 pounds at 35 years of age, Mr. USA! Power, strength!" The crowd goes crazy.

"Scrap!"

I get into my stance and instead of fighting he just brags and boast about himself, taunting me.

"So you have, no powers huh? I guess I'll take it easy on you, but I'll remind you to never try to fight in a serious tournament without powers you delusional punk!"

He walks towards me and he's so strong I feel his footsteps under my feet. As he approaches me, I punch him in his stomach but it does nothing to him.

"Oh this is cute.", he says as people laugh at me. "Try again.", he says.

"Joseph, open palm him! Remember what I did to you!", I hear Master Isaiah say.

I jump up to get eye level with him and open palm him in his face. But still, nothing. In desperation, I swing with all I got with multiple punches but it does nothing.

"This is just sad now.", he says as people continue to laugh cheer for him. He then palms my head with one hand and raises me in the air.

"I'm sorry kid.", he whispers to me. He starts squeezing my head and I yell in pain. I keep punching him in the chest but it does nothing. People chant USA and some are recording. It instantly reminds me of when I was getting jumped. I feel myself fading as I keep punching him. Right before I pass out I hear Master Isaiah yell,

"WHERE'S YOUR FAITH JOSEPH!? YOUR FAMILY STILL BELIEVES IN YOU! ME AND NIA DO AS WELL! BUT YOUR FATHER DOES MOST IMPORTANTLY! USE YOUR FAITH…. NOW JOSEPH!!!"

My eyes snap wide open as I feel an adrenaline rush flow through my body. White smoke flows over my entire body.

"The hell?", Mr. USA says. "Your body is heating up, a lot!"

He drops me and I land on my feet. I look at my arms with my eyes wide open and see white smoke around them. I punch him in the stomach. He actually feels it and bends over in pain. People look in shock and the crowd is filled with WOAHS.

"What…is this? You do have a power. What is it!?", he asks.

I just stare at him.

"WHAT IS IT!!", he demands.

"Ze.", I say in a calm but stern voice.

He rises and charges at me and we both rapidly punch and dodge each other.

"This Ze is making me stronger and able to take more punches as well.", I say to myself in my head. "His punches don't hurt as they normally would. I didn't know Ze could toughen my body like this."

I land a kick to his stomach and he stumbles back.

"Let's go Joseph!", Nia yells.

He then yells, "American Clap!"

He claps his hands and it sends a wave of wind to me hitting my face, but It feels like the strongest punch I've ever felt. I fall down and roll back. People cheer, but for both of us now.

"Get up Joseph!", Master Isaiah says. As I rise I see him squatting like he's about to jump. I notice the white smoke around my hand again and remember the Ze ball I threw at Nia. I tighten my hand again and it comes back in my hand.

"American Leg Drop!!", he yells.

He jumps high in the air and sticks one leg out to leg drop me.

"ZE BLAST JOSEPH! DO IT NOW!", Master Isaiah yells.

I release the Ze ball and I aim it straight but curve it up towards him to catch him by surprise. It hits him before he can fall on me and he lands on his knees but rises on his feet quickly. He looks at me in disbelief and Master Isaiah and everyone has a shocked look on their faces.

"You're good Joseph, but this fight is over! You won't survive another American Clap!", Mr. USA says.

The crowd goes crazy as he gets ready to clap again, I charge up another Ze Blast to counter the clap. But I use two hands this time, for more power.

Everyone looks in awe and Mr. USA's eyes widen. I continue to charge it and it gets bigger than last time.

"AMERICAN……CLAPP!", he screams.

"Ze BLASTTT!!", I yell back. I release all the energy I could muster.

As the two forces collide, it explodes and blows us both back and the bystanders. I pass out from the knockback.

I eventually wake up and see Master Isaiah and Nia over me.

"He's up!", Nia says.

"How do I……..keep ending up like this on the ground?", I say.

They both laugh and help me to my feet.

"Did I win?", I ask.

"Um, no.", Master Isaiah says.

I frown in disappointment.

"But, it was a draw, you both were knocked out from the attack and on top of that, you gained everyone's respect.", Nia says.

"Wait, so I didn't lose?!"

"Nope.", Master Isaiah says. "You have another match tomorrow though. Relax and heal up.", he says.

"Hey kid."

We all look up and see Mr. USA walking towards us. He puts his hand out for me to shake it.

"That was one hell of a match, sorry for underestimating you.", he says in his country voice.

I shake his hand and say thank you.

"I haven't had to fight like that in years. That's a nice power you got there, but hey, when you're trained by the GOAT, anything is possible.", he says.

Master Isaiah eyes widens. He has made a point of emphasis that he doesn't want anyone to know that he's Master Isaiah. After Mr. USA says that, people surround us.

"Sorry Isaiah, but if I have to deal with the fans, so do you.", Mr. USA says and walks off. He tells me and Nia to go to the hotel room as people surround him and we do.

We go to the hotel room, take showers, and change. We both sit and relax and watch TV.

"We both did good today. I'm proud of us both.", Nia says.

"Yea but at least you don't have to fight tomorrow. I still have to win.", I say.

"Yea but you survived Mr. USA, not too many people can say that." She looks at my face and can see it all. "Hey, you need to relax, You're too tense right now."

"That's coming from you? Remember when we first arrived at Master Isaiah's house and you flipped me because I wasn't ready? Now you want me to relax?"

"Yep.", she says.

I look back at the TV and ignore her advice. I can tell she's in a good mood right now, but I can't say the same about myself. She turns it off.

"Look, while we're here lets enjoy it. Remember when I said we can go out for lunch? Let's go out and eat." She gets up and leads me to the door.

"Is this a date?", I ask.

"Look don't drag it out and no. Come on now Joseph!", she says with frustration.

"Ok, ok I'm coming."

We go to a restaurant near the hotel and show are cards that says we are with the exhibition and get in for free. We sit down and eat and enjoy each other's company.

"So you're telling me you never played a video game before, like never?", I ask her.

"Nope, never in my life. I told you I had a rough childhood."

"I did too. We're poor as hell but I still got a GameCube and a Wii.", I say.

We laugh.

"Well you said you never had a girlfriend before. Maybe if you wasn't on the game all the time you could have pulled someone."

She laughs, and I chuckle a bit.

"I just never met anyone that I was interested in. Yea some were pretty, but I just didn't like them once I really got to know them.", I say.

"Yea I guess that's right. I've dated some guys that I regret myself.", she says.

We both laugh. Then a long pause of silence hits the table. We stare at each other, then away, then back, then away again.

"What about now though?", she asks.

I look up and we both stare at each other.

"Nah…..it's different this time.", I say.

"Yea….I think so too.", she says.

We both look at each other in the eyes and simultaneously lean forward and kiss. As she leans back she smiles, and so do I.

"Joseph…I…I'm not going to lie, at first I thought you were weak and crazy…but after seeing how you kept pursuing and pushing yourself…I…I've had this feeling. I wanted to ignore it and focus on winning like you but…I can't suppress it anymore. Even now. You know you still have to win and although you're a bit tense, I like how committed you are.", she tells me while playing with her hair.

"I've always kind of liked you Nia. From the first day I saw you at the park. I always thought you were pretty but now after spending time with you, I see how strong you are as well. As a fighter and a person. You're one of the main reasons I keep pushing myself to newer heights. Hell, I still do.", I tell her.

She starts to smile and it makes me smile. We both continue our food and laugh it up.

We both walk back to the hotel. I never felt like this before, and it seems like we both can't stop staring at each other. I've always kind of wanted to date Nia, but this is deeper than I think either one of us anticipated.

As we enter the hotel room and kiss again, the lights turns on and it's Master Isaiah on the couch, catching us like a parent catching their child come home late.

"Well, well, well. What do we have here?", he asks like a detective.

Both of our black faces turn red.

"I thought you two were out training but it seems like you two were on a date huh?"

"Look Master Isaiah I'm sorry…", I start to say but he interrupts me.

"No, it's fine. I knew this would probably happen eventually."

"Really, I didn't.", Nia says. I look at her with a slight smile but roll my eyes.

"Well I did. As long as you two stay focused and continue to work hard, I don't mind it. Joseph you still have to win tomorrow. Put in work."

"Yessir." I say. I follow Nia to her room but Master Isaiah stops me.

"Um no sir. Get your ass in the living room and go to sleep. I may be getting old but I ain't dumb now."

He slaps me on the back of the head and we all go to sleep.

Chapter 9. Next Gen Rivals!

The next morning we wake up, Nia walks out her room and smiles at me but Master Isaiah nips that in the bud quickly. I don't think he minds us being together, but he wants us to focus for the tournament, especially me since I still need to win. We dress up in our fighting clothes, eat, and head to the event room. I leave to go train in one of the training rooms. I punch one of the dummies and close my eyes to try to activate my Ze again. I need to learn how to use my power on command fast.

White smoke appears around me again. I try to remember what causes it to stay. I think me when I'm focused and with my faith up high is what triggers it. I look in the mirror at myself with all the white glow smoke around me. My eyes are also white.

"Damn, I look cool!", I say to myself. Some of the other fighters in there look at me like a weirdo and laugh at me because I talked to myself. My face gets as red as it possibly could with me being black and I walk out.

I enter back into the main event to see some fights. But I end up with my eyes stuck on the board. Nia approaches me.

"What's the matter?", she asks.

"I fight Haru today! The level 65 Ze user."

"Oh.", she says. "You got a gameplan?"

"No but I'm going to win. This is personal." I say.

"Hey, Joseph!" We hear a country voice calling my name. It's Mr. USA. I'm guessing people got use to him being around so not a lot of people surround him as much. He puts his hand out for me to shake it again and I do.

"I came here to warn you about your opponent.", he says.

"I already know.", I interrupt.

"Oh, guess I was late. After I won my match I wanted to warn you about him so you could make it to the tournament so I can fight you again."

"Excuse me?", Nia says.

"No, no it's not in disrespect, I just want to fight you again. Yesterday was one of the best fights in my life and I need it again!", he says in excitement.

"Oh, thank you." I say.

"Also, who's she. A lady friend?", he says suggesting something.

"Um….", I say. I don't know our label yet.

"Yes.", Nia interrupts.

Lady friend it is.

"Hey, I notice you now, you're Nia. I heard you beat Killer Carlos which is tough to do. Congratulations.", he says.

"Thank you, and also I can give you a better fight than Joseph can.", Nia tells him.

"Oh we'll see one day.", he says.

"Anyways Haru has Ze and he's the best at it. I'm assuming you have that as well. Just like Isaiah and Jiro. Look he'll try to distract you with his fighting, it's really good. Then when you think you got him, BAM! He hits you with a Ze attack and you're done. Watch out for him and win!"

"Yes…sir..", I say not knowing what to call him.

"Please, call me Mr. USA!", he shouts.

People rush towards him as he yells.

"Damn it!", he says as he runs off.

"Well at least you made a new friend who also is one of the richest, most popular person in the world.", Nia says. We both laugh and watch a match behind us.

We see one match with this guy named Taz. He's from Australia and he turns into a beast with brown fur and a long tail. It's kind of hard to beat him with his sharp claws and fast, beast like movements. He spins fast like the cartoon character and has acid spit. There's something sinister about him though and he destroys his opponent easily.

We watch another match with a South African girl named Kaya. She has long spears with no powers, but she uses them perfectly. She can't be touched and keeps distance with her spears with ease.

We watch more matches and see one with Mr. Russia, who is pretty much Mr. USA, but Russian. He destroys his opponent easily too. Then him and Mr. USA get into a tense stare down and they square up but people and others with powers help calm down the situation. Then my match comes up.

Me, Nia, and Master Isaiah walk to our match area and with the fight I had yesterday against Mr. USA, I've gained a little of a fan following and people follow to watch. Nia has fans too and of course Master Isaiah does so we have a lot of attention on us. But Haru or Jiro aren't here yet.

People look around in confusion. I get hope, hoping it's a no show and I automatically win, or at least fight someone weaker. But sadly, they show up. I see Jiro in his robe and a guy next to him who I assuming is Haru.

He's built just a little bit stronger than me and has a white training robe with no sleeves. On the back it has Japanese letters on it that I think is for a clan. He walks to the match area and stares me down but I don't back down. I stare him down back. I look to the side and see Master Isaiah and Jiro staring each other down. People surround the two legends as they stare intensely at each other.

"Here we are again my friend.", Jiro says to Master Isaiah.

"Don't start with me!", Master Isaiah response back.

"Oh calm down, it's not about us anymore!" He points to me and Haru.

"It's about them. The next gen rivals!", he says.

"Well….at least if Haru wins, the country won't stop him from getting his rematch." Master Isaiah says as he walks away with Nia to my corner.

"You will fail.", Haru tells me.

"You could have at least shook my hand before the trash talk.", I tell him.

"You're a dishonor to Ze Power.", he says.

"Says the guy who got it the stolen way. Must've felt good having Jiro pass it down to you huh?", I say back. He must not have known that I knew the truth.

He chuckles and puts on his black elbow pads.

"We'll see who's the best at Ze Power.", he says.

The announcer calls the match.

"From Memphis Tennessee, at 6'0 weighing 174 pounds at 18 years of age, Joseph! Power, Ze Power!"

People now cheer for me.

"From Tokyo Japan, at 6'2 weighing 181 pounds at 20 years of age, Haru! Power, Ze Power! We both walk up to each other. "Scrap!", the announcer yells.

People chant and are excited to see this fight. Other matches even go on pause to see ours. For a second we just stare at each other. It's crazy, because I have never met this guy ever in my life, but I feel a connection with him. That this goes back way farther than us. This is the next Isaiah vs Jiro. The next gen rival and only one of us can come out as the winner.

I don't hesitate and I make the first quick punch and he dodges it. He then swings and I duck and roll behind him. He tries to hit me with a jump kick and I avoid that as well but as I turn around after I dodge his attack, I hear a loud ,"ZE Power!"

I turn around to see a big Ze blast right in front of my face. I barely duck under it and it explodes when it hits the wall, destroying it. He looks at the surprised look on my face and chuckles.

"I'm way stronger than that wall punk!", I tell him and charge up an attack of my own. But as I tighten up my arm, he charges at me quickly and punches me at least five times in my face.

I fall back as people chant and, "OOOO" and, "Ahhhhh."

"You will fail.", he says to me again.

"Shut up!", I respond as I get to my feet, but he gives me no time to recover. He picks me up and tosses me across the mat.

"Get up Joseph!" Master Isaiah yells.

"You got this, remember this is personal!", Nia says.

"WIN BOY, FOR OUR GREAT NATION JOSEPH!!!", Mr. USA screams in Master Isaiah and Nia's ear.

I stumble to my feet. And he charges at me again but this time I trip him. As he's on the ground, I remember when I got jumped and I punch him directly in his eye. It may be a dirty move, but I'm here to win.

"Yes Joseph!", Master Isaiah yells. Then I hear Jiro.

"HARU! Failure is not an option! Stop playing and end him or I'll end you!", he tells Haru.

Haru rises to his feet.

"You….will…fail!"

He starts to glow with white smoke. I start to do the same.

"Focus, and faith.", I tell myself.

We charge at each other and trade attacks and blows. Both of us start to bleed badly but neither of us give in. This is pure scrapping. He backs away and throws another blast at me and I throw one back and they explode. People chant, cheer, and yell. We go back to punching and dodging. He sweeps me from my feet and kicks me back. He then throws five Ze blasts at me. I dodge four of them, but the last one hits me, knocking me to the ground hard.

"JOSEPH!", Master Isaiah and Nia yell.

I fade in and out of consciousness but before the announcer calls the match, I get up. I know if I take another hit like that, I'm done.

"Finish him now Haru! NOW!!!", I hear Jiro yell.

His Ze is way stronger than mines but is he smarter than me? He rushes towards me yelling and swings but I grab his punch and head bud him in his other eye. He lets out a painful yell. The crowd is more and more invested in this fight more than I thought they would be. And I am too.

As he tries to recover I charge a Ze attack with both of my hands instead of just one to try to gain more power. "ZE…BLAST!!!", I yell and with my hand glowing, I hit him with all I got. But that wasn't what I was going for.

I faked him! He thought I was going for a blast when it was the punch that I hit him with. Ze makes it more powerful and to my surprise, it knocks him out unconscious.

"Winner, Joseph!", the announcer calls. The watching spectators cheer and clap while analyst look with their mouth wide open in shock. People cheer my name and shout upset, because I wasn't expected to win. Nia rushes to hug me.

"You did it! You made it!", she chants.

Master Isaiah tells me good job and I can tell he's proud of me. "I told you, I'd teach you everything you need to know. But it's up to you to use it. I'm proud of you."

I give him a hug. "Congratulations, you made it Joseph", he says. Nia jumps in on the hug and so does Mr. USA. He squeezes us a little too tight though.

"That's my boy! That's that American pride in you! Now we can fight again in the tournament!", he yells with passion.

"Um…yea.", I say. I guess me and Mr. USA are somewhat friends or rivals I guess. I have to tell Derrick and Frank when I get back home.

Haru rises and approaches me. He sticks his hand out to shake it and I do.

"Good match.", he says, "But next time I will win, I promise."

"I'll be waiting on it.", I say.

"I shouldn't have underestimated you Joseph. You tricked me with that punch. But it's always the rematch that will tell a different story.", he tells me.

He smirks and walks towards an angry Jiro, who is staring down Master Isaiah and me.

I try not to think about what he said too much. I just try to enjoy my victory and the rest of my time in California. And I do.

Chapter 10. To Answer All Your Questions…

We arrive back in Memphis and as we enter Master Isaiah's house, all of us fall out on the couch.

"So, we actually did it.", I say.

"Yea….we did.", Nia responds.

"Yea but it's not over yet. It's just began and now both of you have targets on your back so you have to fight and get even stronger. We'll keep training. We have a month and a half till the tournament.", Master Isaiah tells us.

"Yessir.", we both say.

"I'm going to call my mom real quick.", I say. Nia heads to the backyard to warm up and Master Isaiah heads back to his room.

"Momma, you won't believe this but I've been qualified for the tournament! I got in!", I tell her. I hear her and Savannah scream in excitement. They yell and run around the house for about five minutes straight. I try to calm them down but it doesn't work. They even get Bishop all excited and he joins them. I even hear some neighbors ask if they are okay.

"I'm so proud of you Joseph! I really am!", she says.

"Thanks momma. Sorry I haven't been calling daily anymore. I need to talk to you guys more.", I say.

"Don't worry about us. You keep doing your thing and you come back with that money. But most importantly safe."

"I'll try not to. How have you been health wise momma?", I ask.

"I'm actually getting a little bit better but I had to take off work. Savannah has gotten a job for now and we get help from neighbors."

"How is she handling school and a job?", I ask.

"Boy didn't I tell you don't worry about us? We'll be fine.", she says.

"I know, it's just hard not to." I hear Bishop barking in the background again. "Oh damn, who made him upset now?", I ask.

We both laugh.

Then suddenly I hear a loud scream. It's a loud, banshee like scream of pain and horror. It comes from the backyard and I know it's Nia.

"I'll call you back momma!"

I hang up the phone and me and Master Isaiah rush to the backyard. He must've heard it too. It was hard not to.

We see Nia in the back on her knees crying in anger, sorrow, and pain. She yells uncontrollably.

"Nia! What happened?", I ask.

"Did you hurt something?", Master Isaiah asks.

"No….my….my parents called…..they found my sister…….they found her dead……dead…..dead……..", she says, struggling to get it out while crying uncontrollably.

"Oh damn.", I say in sadness.

I can't express or even explain the pain that she must be feeling. I know she was very crazy about her big sister.

"She…..she killed herself. She……she sent me a text message too during the tournament that……I didn't….read or open……..she said………she failed………", she cries.

"Nia, come inside.", Master Isaiah says.

I try to pick her up and help her in but she yanks away from me.

"It's my fault! It is!", she yells.

"Don't say that!", I say.

"IT IS!!!", she shouts even louder. "I should've been there! I shouldn't be here! I should've been with her when I KNEW she needed me! But instead I'm off, lollygagging fighting people thinking I can actually win this STUPID tournament! This isn't real life! She dealt with real life and I'm here living like I'm in a damn video game with you two!"

"Nia…", I say sadly.

"I'm out of here! Joseph…good luck but remember, this isn't real life. We don't have good endings and life isn't a damn fairytale! I'm sorry for wasting your time Master Isaiah and Joseph, but I can't waste my time on this. This isn't that important to me anymore." She walks off.

"Nia!", I try to chase after her but Master Isaiah holds me back. Before she leaves I ask her something.

"So beating Carlos and standing up for women is nothing?! Is Master Isaiah nothing!? Am I nothing!? What about faith, is that nothing!? I thought you wanted this for you and your sister...", I ask her in desperation.

"MY SISTER IS GONE JOSEPH!!!", she screams.

The backyard fills with a dreaded silence. I know Nia is hurt. More than I was when my father died.

"And to answer all your questions at once Joseph, yes. This is nothing, and now that my sister is gone, I'm nothing."

She walks in the house, packs her things, and exits the front door. I try to stop her and I yell her name but she ignores me. Master Isaiah stops me in the front yard.

"She needs space Joseph. Let her have that right now.", he tells me.

I watch her walk down the street, until she fades away, and I don't see her anymore.

I sit on the couch staring at the wall thinking how everything changed so fast. One minute we're all on top of the world, the next, down back in hell. Master Isaiah comes over and puts his hands on my shoulder and tears start to roll down my face.

I know I have to keep going, but it's going to be way harder with Nia gone. I know it's selfish to say or even think because her sister just died, but I really wish she didn't say that this was all nothing to her. Most importantly, me. I'm going to miss her, and that's what hurts the most. Now I do this for my mother, sister, Master Isaiah, my father, and now Nia.

I can't even get any sleep tonight. My head is going in circles on how fast life just changed. But there's a part of me that understands. If Savannah or my mother just died, I'd probably do and say the same thing. But that realization doesn't make it hurt any less.

I lie on the couch hoping to hear a knock on it, but don't. I never felt a heartbreak before, but I feel like this is way worse and it just won't go away, not even a little. It all feels fake.

I'm sad because she's gone, and that her sister passed the way she did. I know the only way I'll get over this is to sadly get over her and forget her, but I can't. I'll have to erase Nia from my mind to win this tournament, and sadly, I have no other choice.

Me and Master Isaiah train the next day. He can clearly see that I'm not in the mood and he stops our jog on the bridge.

"You notice where we are kid?", he asks me.

I look around and it hits me. We're on the same bridge where my father died right in front of me. I remember it like it was yesterday.

"License and registration sir.", the officer asked.

"Why am I being pulled over officer?", my dad asked.

"License and registration sir!", the officer said with more aggression.

 More officers arrive.

"Just show them Johnny.", my momma said.

Now there are two officers on the passenger side staring at my momma. One looks in the back at me and I'll never forget his mean face that haunts me to this day. My father shows license and registration.

"Any weapons in the vehicle sir?", the officer asked.

"Why does that matter? You can't just go from license and registration to is there a weapon.", my dad said while clearly irritated.

The other officer that mean mugged me yells, "Is there a weapon in the vehicle!"

"Yes the hell there is! And I'm registered to have it damn it! To protect me from these crazy people out here and you!", my dad says in anger.

"Get out the car now!", the mean mug officer ordered.

They tussle and drag my father out the car while my mom yells and I cry for my daddy. Savannah is a newborn and is just crying due to the commotion, but I know she also knew something bad was happening.

We see them drag him and toss him on the police car parked in front of us. A lot of cuss words are being said from both sides.

They start to beat him and my mom yells and jumps out of the car to help as much as she can. She's tackled hard and gets cuffed on the ground.

My dad, being any husband who sees their wife and kids in danger, snaps and rushes to the cop who's on my mother. Then……

POW POW!!!

I see my father fall and my mother cry louder than anyone or anything I've heard in my life.

Later I found out they thought my dad was someone who was suspected for a double murder, which is bull crap because they saw his license. To put it blunt, they just wanted to beat another black man down. And sadly they got something better for them, they killed one. My father.

I don't even remember if they were found guilty or not but I don't give a damn. They can't bring my father back so it doesn't matter to me. The only thing I want for them is to rot in hell, but sadly I've been living in hell ever since then.

"Why are we here!", I ask Master Isaiah in frustration.

"To show you how far you've come in life kid. I remember crying myself after hearing about it. You started and have lived in hell your entire life, and now you're about to make a change, and you don't even know it. Use your pain to strengthen your Ze Joseph.", he tells me.

We both look into the river. We just watch as the waves move by, the birds fly by, and the fish swim by.

"This is just another part of your story kid. Every one of us have our own books and this is yours. It's up to you to make it a happy ending. And hopefully, Nia finds that out too."

"You're right.", I say.

"You know even though Nia isn't here, she'll still be at home cheering you on.", he tells me.

"I know but it still sucks. I wanted both of us to fight and make it.", I say.

"Yeah I did too, but everything in life happens for a reason kid. Whether it's good or bad, it's up to you to make a positive next move."

We both just stare into the city of Memphis.

"Also, you two aren't done yet.", he says.

"What do you mean?", I ask.

"I'm not going to say Nia loves you or anything corny like that, but I do know she cares for you a lot. She's been looking over you your whole time here. She even got mad at me because she thought I was being too tough on you. She's not going to be gone forever." , he assures me.

I smirk a little bit.

"Yea I know, I just hope it's not too late."

Chapter 11. Hometown Hero

Me and Master Isaiah train for the remaining weeks leading up to the tournament. It's hard, but I manage to make it without Nia. With her presence missing, it feels like our training is lacking or not fulfilled.

After me and Master Isaiah finish our jogs and fighting in the backyard, I sit on his front porch stairs and just view the beautiful site. It's warm, and people jog and birds and squirrels roam around.

I take a deep inhale and exhale. As I do, I feel the Ze expanding throughout my body.

Master Isaiah joins me and takes a seat on the front porch with me.

"Enjoying the view kid?", Master Isaiah asks me.

"Yea. Just taking it easy for now.", I tell him.

We both just sit and watch and wave at the people who walk by us. Today is oddly very peaceful and calm. Usually all that can be heard around here are police sirens, gunshots, and cars on the interstate.

While we sit and relish in the joyful afternoon, a woman notices me.

"Hey, you're that Joseph kid! From the Time to Scrap tournament, right?", she asks me.

She seems like a college girl. She's black and very pretty. It catches me totally by surprise.

"Yea...that's me.", I say, trying to keep myself together.

"I heard about your fight in the exhibition against Mr. USA. It was insane!", she says.

"Oh, thank you.", I say wholesomely.

"You keep it up and win the tournament and represent Memphis proudly. Also, can I please get a picture?", she asks.

I agree and get up to take a picture with her. I guess I've been so focused on training and winning this tournament that I forgot about the celebrity part that comes with it.

After the 3rd picture we take, she smiles and continues her jog.

"See, I told you that you'd make a change.", Master Isaiah tells me.

"I haven't done anything yet though.", I tell him.

"Yea, but people already know about you. You have their trust and respect, and most importantly, they want you to represent them. It doesn't get any more prideful than that."

"I guess so.", I say.

Even though he's not lying, I still feel like I have to prove myself. I've only beaten Haru and now I know I have a target on my back from other fighters. And I still need to win so I can finally get me and my family out of hell.

BANG! BANG!

Me and Master Isaiah both jump as we hear the loud bang noise. We can both easily tell it's from downtown.

"The hell was that!?", Master Isaiah asks.

"I don't know!", I say.

I then bolt straight towards downtown Memphis. Master Isaiah follows me. We both run as fast as we possibly can. Although we aren't allowed to use our powers, if it comes to it in order to save a life, I will without a doubt.

As we get closer and closer to downtown, we hear and see more and more people running away and screaming. There's smoke from a building that seems to cover the entire area.

When we finally arrive at the scene, we see a building has exploded. It's an abandoned building, but people, debris, and smoke are everywhere.

"Joseph! Help me clear the area!", Master Isaiah demands me.

"Yessir!"

I notice some people on the sidewalk in pain. I rush over to them to help them. I put two people on my back and rush them to safety.

As I return to help more people, I notice a huge ass white man in a blue and yellow bodysuit. He has a thick beard and dull black eyes. He jumps from the building and lands in the street, destroying it with his strength.

"Agh, finally! I've finally found you!", he says.

"Who the hell are you!?", I ask.

"The name is Quake. I've been looking for you Joseph! I was originally searching for Mr. USA to prove my true strength, but once I found out he had a draw with you, I couldn't resist the chance to fight! Plus, you're an easier man to get access to!", he says.

"If you wanted a fight you could've asked, but you instead harmed innocent people!", I yell.

"It was an easy way to get your attention. I knew you were from Memphis so you would have no choice but to fight me!"

"I see you're a man that wants the easy way out! Fine, I'll easily kick your ass!", I tell him.

"Go ahead and try!"

"Joseph! Don't waste your time! You have a tournament coming up!", Master Isaiah tells me.

"This one will be quick Master.", I assure him.

"You cocky bastard! Let's fight!!!", Quake says.

He runs towards me and just like Mr. USA, I can feel every step he takes under me. He charges at me with his shoulders, but I leap right over him. He turns around in confusion and when he does, I kick him in the side of his face.

He steps back a little but doesn't seem too shaken by it.

"You're fast huh!?", he asks.

"Na, just faster than you!", I tell him.

He gets mad but I punch him twice in the body hard. Once again, it doesn't shake him, and he grabs me by my shirt.

"Try harder than that kid!", he says.

He then holds me up by squeezing my shoulders. He's about the same height as Mr. USA, but he's built like a giant boulder. And I yell loudly in pain as he squeezes my shoulders.

He finally releases me and throws me to the ground.

"EARTHQUAKE!!!", I hear him yell.

He jumps high into the air and aims for me. If he lands on me, he'll kill me, and it's not even up for question.

I roll out of the way as soon as he lands on the ground, but the ground does shake and the buildings start to crumble again. Master Isaiah is still moving quickly to help people out the way, but if I don't hurry and end this, it could be too late.

Quake doesn't give up even though he missed. He gets up and stares at me.

"Rolling Boulder!", he yells.

He rolls towards me like a hedgehog and moves fast for such a big guy.

"Ze Blast!", I yell as I blast Ze at him.

It doesn't stop him though. It slows him down, but he keeps moving.

"Ha! Try again!", he yells while still rolling.

"No problem, Ze Blast!!!" I yell, releasing even more power.

He struggles, but he keeps on moving.

I charge more Ze in my other hand as I keep the blast going and he gets closer to me. I can tell he thinks he's won.

"It's over punk!", he yells.

"Yea it is!", I yell back at him.

As soon as he gets close enough to me, I punch him with my other hand charge with Ze Power.

I catch him right in his stomach and he pauses in pain.

"You...you bastard!", he says.

He grabs his stomach and falls to the ground. I stand over him with one foot on his big stomach.

"See, if you would have just asked or entered the tournament this could've been fun. But now you have to go to jail.", I tell Quake.

All he can do is moan and groan in pain on the ground.

About a couple minutes later, the police and CHF finally arrive.

"Damn it! It's Quake again!", one of the CHF members say as they land from the sky.

"Yea, but it seems he's already been taken care of.", another officer says while looking at me.

"So…sorry sir.", I say as I slowly step off Quake. "He was just destroying everything and I acted fast and…", I start to say. The officer interrupts me though.

"No, no it's fine. Actually, I'm impressed. He's been causing terror in different cities across the country, and we couldn't ever stop him. Not without extra, extra back up anyways. I'll cut you some slack this time.", he tells me.

"Thank you, officer.", I say with a smile. I'd never thought I would be thanking an officer ever in my life.

"No problem. Plus, you have a tournament to win kid. Now go get some rest."

I smile harder than I have in a long time. I haven't smiled like this since Nia left.

They put Quake in special cuffs and take him away. I go to find Master Isaiah who's communicating with the ambulance team. Once he's done, he walks towards me and says it's time to go home.

As we leave and walk back home, people chant and clap for me. Some wish me luck for the tournament and others ask for a picture. I just smile through it all, and I promise to myself that I'll win this tournament, for Memphis.

But also, for Nia.

Chapter 12. The Tournament Begins

It's been hard, but me and Master Isaiah have trained for the last month and a half hard. But it's finally time for the tournament to begin. We pack our things and get ready for the tournament. But before we leave, Master Isaiah tells me something.

"Do this, for Nia son. You can win. You are ready." He smiles with a look of a proud father.

"Yessir.", I say. After everything I've been through, it's now finally time. It's time to scrap. The butterflies are definitely in my stomach, but I'm also very excited and ready.

We fly to the tournament meet up where all the fighters are. But the whole time, I can't get Nia out of my head. I don't see her here, which hurts. As I look around and see the amazing fighters, I get more and more sadder. This is what we both hoped for.

A few people come up to me and recognize me from the exhibition. They ask for autographs, and I smile a little, but when they leave, it goes away.

"Ugh! Just forget about it! I have to move on to win!", I say to myself loudly.

"What's the matter kid, someone left you broken?"

I hear that southern country voice and I know exactly who it is.

"Oh, I bet it was that Nia girl huh?", he guesses.

"Not now Mr. USA.", I say not in the mood. How did he find out so fast?

"Well, you better forget about her if you want to win! I can't fight you when you're a shattered, broken, half of a man! You need to be at your best so I can beat you at your best! Forget about her!", he tells me.

"I've tried, and I can't." I look down and try to hold back the tears. "We trained and got to know each other." The flashbacks of our fights, our training, our date, our kiss. I can't clear my mind.

"Oh boy, this is worse than I thought.", Mr. USA says.

He searches the room. "Hey! You see that tall lanky man over there?" He points to an African man dripped out in gold jewelry and a black and purple tux. He's got like a purplish ball thing floating in his hands.

"He's Magic Moses. His power is Magic, of course. He can clear your mind and make it to where you never even met this girl. Come on."

He drags me over to him against my will. It sounds like a perfect plan but, I don't know if I want to forget her…forever.

"Ah, what brings you over USA?", Moses asks.

"Look I need a favor. You see this guy got dumped and he needs to forget about his old gal so he can focus on this tournament so I can fight him at his best.", he says.

"Yea, or I could beat him and eliminate him with ease since his mind is a fog.", Moses says.

"Yea, he's that Joseph guy. I heard about you at the exhibition.", Kaya says. She's the one at the tournament who had the spears.

"I heard he's pretty good. He has to be if he beat Haru his first fight.", she says.

"He is, which is why if he's going to be a crybaby punk, then we can just beat him with ease.", Magic Moses says.

"Now where's the fun and honor in that Moses?", Mr. USA ask.

"This is the Time to Scrap Tournament USA, honor means nothing. It's about winning."

"Pleeeeasssssseeee! Do it for me.", Mr. USA begs.

"Agh, fine. But you owe me.", Magic Moses agrees.

"Yes! Thank you Moses!", Mr. USA says happily.

"Do you wish to forget about this girl son? It's that Nia girl, right?", Kaya asks me.

"Yes.", I say sadly.

"Yea she's very good too.", Kaya says.

"Really?", Magic Moses asks.

"Yea. Her hair move is so unique and unpredictable. I saw how close you two were at the exhibition. Are you sure you want to forget her? You may not ever remember her again.", she explains.

"I'm never going to see her again, so I guess it doesn't matter.", I say hopelessly.

"Oh boy, he is broken. What's her name again? That's all I need, and then you'll forget all about anyone with that name.", he says.

I hesitate for a second but respond.

"Nia…"

He does some magic stuff with his hands and the purple orbs float and spin around my head very fast. When they stop, my head nods hard.

"You good kid?", Mr. USA asks.

I feel so confused out of nowhere now. It takes me a second to remember where I am and what's going on. I even stumble a bit.

"Um, I think. I think, I think I was sad about something, but I can't remember anymore.", I say as I start to feel better.

"Yes! It worked! Thank you Moses!", Mr. USA says.

"Just remember, you owe me USA.", Magic Moses tells him.

"Of course!", he responds.

Magic Moses and Kaya walks away.

"Now Joseph, are you ready to scrap!?", Mr. USA asks with energy.

"Of course I am, why would I be here if I wasn't? And this time it'll be no tie!", I say.

"Ha, that's the spirit!"

He walks off with excitement, but I'm still confused on what just happened.

I feel another hand on my shoulder. I turn around and to my surprise it's Haru.

"Joseph.", he says. "Good to see you."

"Oh, so you made it huh?", I ask.

"Well after losing to you, I took my next match seriously and won in five seconds."

"Five? Wow, you're one tough badass Haru." He chuckles.

"You'll find out for real this time, that's if you can get past my cousin, Akio."

"I will, and I'll be waiting on you." He smirks and walks off.

Master Isaiah finds me and directs me to the stage with everyone else. There is an announcer on the stage.

"Ladies and gentlemen it is now the time you've all been waiting for! Welcome to The Time to Scrap Tournament!"

People cheer and I instantly remember where I am. It feels unreal as I see cameras everywhere and I feel happiness and adrenaline. I'm on TV. I made it! Little Joseph from Memphis, Tennessee. I hope everyone back at home notices me.

"Now the first fight will be tomorrow in Memphis, Tennessee. Joseph vs Akio!", the announcer says.

People cheer for me and the match itself. I can't believe I have the first match, and it's in my hometown.

"It'll then be followed by Mr. USA vs Austin U.K. in Dallas Texas, and lastly Taz vs Kaya in Australia! That will be day one of The Time to Scrap Tournament! Tune in tomorrow for the fight!"

I hear the commentators announce fighters that they think will win. I hear one of them bring up Killer Carlos. He must be tough for people to mention him, but I'm not too worried.

A lot of other names are brought up too. Like Haru, Polar Zero, and to my surprise, even mines. One of them go on though about how it's impossible for Chen to lose, a fighter from China. Usually I'd be worried about all this competition, but I honestly think I can hold my own against any fighter here.

As the people start to scatter again, Mr. USA runs up to me.

"Well kid, you better win, so I can meet you in a match!", he tells me.

"Don't worry about that mate! You'll have to deal with me first!"

A man in a British military theme outfit walks to us. He even has the tall furry black hat thing. This must be Austin U.K.

"Oh please, what's water to muscle?", Mr. USA says not taking him seriously.

"Oh, you'll find out tomorrow mate.", he laughs.

"Oh we'll see about that!", Mr. USA responds back.

"Both of you are foolish if you think you're winning this tournament! I am!", Mr. Russia interrupts.

"I beat you once Russia, I'll do it again damn it!", Mr. USA says. He's very serious, and aggressive towards Mr. Russia. I feel like I'm missing something from these two.

"We both know you escaped me Mr. USA! Not beat me! And you never have or will beat me Austin! I am the world's strongest man and best fighter!", Mr. Russia says.

All three of them get very close like they are about to fight right here, right now. Some people even record with their phones and chant scrap. Other fighters and tournament officials struggle to separate all three of them.

I get out of their drama and look for Master Isaiah through the sea of people.

People walk up to me asking for more autographs and I keep getting lost. I even start to yell for Master Isaiah, but it's pointless because it's so loud here.

"Joseph! Joseph! Joseph!"

I hear someone calling me. I turn around and see a pretty black girl with four very long pigtail braids going past her knees.

She runs up to me and gives me a hug. I try not to blush, but I look around in confusion.

She let's go and looks at me with disappointment, like she wanted a hug back.

"Joseph…. I'm…. I'm sorry. I was upset and I didn't mean everything I said. I do care for this. For Master Isaiah. And for you. She grabs my hand.

"Um……what?", I ask in confusion. I'm so lost that it scares me. Maybe she's pranking me? Or has me confused with someone else.

"Are you ok?", she asks. "What's wrong with you?"

Well, it doesn't seem like this is a prank. She's dead serious.

"Um, I think you have the wrong person, I'm sorry.", I tell her.

I'm so lost and confused right now.

"Joseph, what the hell is wrong with you? It's me, Nia! I know it's been a while, but it hasn't been that long.

"I'm sorry, I have to go, Nia. Hopefully you find who you're looking for.", I tell her.

I see tears start to come down her face. I try to walk away slowly.

"Joseph!", she cries.

"Please stop! I'm sorry!", she pleads causing attention.

I see Master Isaiah running towards us.

"Master Isaiah, I've been looking for you!", I say.

"Well yea, but I saw Nia here. I told her you were here, and she ran off searching for you without me. Now that she's here, you both can focus up and give it your all, right?"

He looks at her crying and sees the lost and confused look on my face.

"What's wrong now?", he asks.

"I don't even know.", I say starting to get frustrated.

"He's acting like he doesn't know me! Like we never met before!", she starts to cry again.

Master Isaiah grabs me by my shirt and lifts me off the ground.

"The hell are you doing boy!", he says quietly but stern.

"Master Isaiah, I've never met her ever in my life! I don't know who she is or why she's acting like this.", I tell him.

I'm so confused and worried, but this Nia girl is crazy and it's pissing me off. He looks at Nia, then he scans my face intensely. He puts me down and lets out a deep sigh.

"Nia get up and stop crying. It's obvious he's under some type of influence from someone or something. Once we find out, things will go back to normal. But for now I need you both to focus up. My goodness I came for a fight, not some high school romance drama. Now can we ready up!?"

"Yessir!", I say. Nia stares at me with a sad look on her face.

"Nia, we'll fix him. I promise.", he tells her.

"Yessir.", she says quietly.

"Why do I have to be fix for?", I ask with an offended voice.

The event finally ends, and Nia agrees to come to Memphis with us. On our way back home in the car, Nia hits me with an interrogation of questions.

"How do you not remember me?", she asks starting to get mad.

"I don't know, and I've never met you before.", I tell her trying to ignore her.

"Yes you have dumbass! We trained and fought against each other. I saved you from those gang members fool!", she says.

"No, you didn't. Master Isaiah did fool!", I respond.

She swings her hair and slaps me in the face.

"The hell is wrong with you! That hurt!", I yell.

"You're what the hell is wrong with me you dumbass!", she yells back.

"BOTH OF YOU ARE DRIVING ME CRAZY! BE QUIET UNTIL WE GET TO MY HOUSE!!!", Master Isaiah yells. He's never yelled this loud at me.

Me and Nia both look out the window for the rest of the drive in the backseat. I can hear her crying a little again and it pisses me off. I don't know her, and she's really distracting me from my fight. I'll have to forget about her and move on to win.

"Nia, listen sweetie. We'll fix Joseph, I promise. Something is wrong with him, but right now we can't do nothing about it. Okay?", Master Isaiah asks her.

"Okay."

"Ain't a damn thing wrong with me.", I mumble under my breath.

"Joseph, shut the hell up respectfully. Yes there is.", he says.

The rest of the car ride is silent, and we finally make it back to Master Isaiah's house. I throw my things on the floor and lay right on the couch. I'm so tired that I don't even eat. I get some rest for my big fight tomorrow against Akio.

As I fall asleep, I see Nia lay down on the other couch. I act like I'm sleep, but I can still hear her crying a little bit. I force myself to sleep. I'm not going to let this crazy girl get in my way from winning. Or distract me anymore. I must win, for me, Master Isaiah, and most importantly my mom and Savannah.

The next day comes and it's finally time.

I get to choose where the fight will take place since it's my hometown. I chose the bridge over the river where the police killed my dad in honor of him.

People from all around the city show up in support. My teachers, other students, all the store owners. It's packed, and I even see my co-worker Derrick who told me about the tournament and my boss Jax.

"Oh my God Joseph, you're ripped now!", Derrick says.

"Give it all you got mane!", Jax says in his Memphis voice.

"Thanks!", I say. It honestly feels good seeing them all again. Especially knowing I didn't rob them.

I see Jamal across the bridge. I run over to him to dap him up.

"Well looks like you not getting jumped ever again.", he says jokingly.

"Yea, yea, well things changed so fast, but me getting jumped was probably the best worst thing to ever happen to me.", I say to him.

Actually, I have to thank Stacy. Technically if it wasn't for her, none of this would be happening. We both laugh.

Nia walks up to us both and my face instantly drops.

"Here's some water and your outfit Joseph.", she says as she hands over a bag with clothes and a gallon of water.

"Thanks…. Nia, right?", I say remembering her name. I guess I'll try to be nice to her. She's very pretty, but still crazy though.

She shakes her head yes in disappointment and gives it to me. She rubs her hand on my shoulder and stares at me, then walks away.

"Forget about Stacy, what's up with Nia? She looks kind of bad.", Jamal says with a grin.

"I don't even know her.", I say.

"Oh come on Joseph. She gave you your fit and rubs your shoulder and she stares into your soul. You know that gal.", he says with confidence.

"No, I really don't.", I say trying to convince him.

"Well if you don't want her I'll be more than happy to take her. She too fine.", he tells me. I roll my eyes.

I pull my fit out the bag. I usually wear a black and white muscle shirt and shorts, but because I'm in Memphis, I wear a color scheme like the Memphis Grizzlies. But their old ones when they were in Canada. I'm not going to lie, it's pretty dope. I have a turquoise muscle shirt with red tape around my elbows and wrist. I wear turquoise shorts with red stripes at the bottom. I also wear a red ninja headband.

A few moments later I see Haru, Jiro and who I'm guessing is Akio. They ready up on the other side of the bridge. People circle around us as the fight gets ready and the announcer gets in the middle of the bridge. There are cameras everywhere and I feel like a pro athlete.

"From Memphis Tennessee, at 6'0 weighing 174 pounds at 18 years of age, Joseph!"

People cheer, roar, and jump. I never felt a feeling like this before. I see the cameras and know people are watching worldwide, but I only care about the people here, my home.

"Power, Ze Power!", the announcer says finishing my attributes.

"And from Tokyo Japan, at 5'9 weighing 159 pounds at 19 years of age, Akio! Power, teleportation!"

Teleportation? That'll be tricky, but I can't lose.

"Now it's Time to Scrap!", the announcer yells as people get hyped.

He wastes no time and charges at me and I anticipate the punch, but he disappears and I feel a hard kick behind me. It knocks me across the ground and people awe in shock. I get up quickly.

"I heard you beat my cousin. You bring dishonor to my family and for that, you'll pay."

"Sure.", I say with a smirk on my face.

I run up to him again and right as I swing, he disappears again. I look behind me and can't see him. I hear someone say look up and I dodge the drop kicked he planned for me.

He must've teleported on the top of the bridge. He's smart.

"Next time you won't escape!", he tells me.

He charges me and I anticipate the teleport but he doesn't and actually combos me with punches and kicks.

I fall back once it ends. People cheer me on my feet. I hear the commentator talking garbage about me calling me overhyped.

I smile as I get up.

"What's so funny?", he asks.

"I've figured you out. No wonder you're not as good as your cousin. You're too easy.", I tell him.

The crowd gets hyped from the trash talk.

"Bluff!", he yells in anger.

It's actually not. He's going to either hit me when he charges towards me or teleport. He relies on his power too much. He charges at me and I grab his arm and flip him on his back. People chant and roar louder.

He gets up and teleports quickly throughout the whole bridge to where I can see him and can't over and over again.

I get in my stance and he appears right in front of me. He swings and I duck under him, but he teleports behind me again and kicks me as hard as he can. I yell in pain.

"Come on Joseph!", I hear Nia yell.

"Stay down!", he tells me.

"Never!", I say. "Now….it's my turn!"

I tighten my body and the white smoke appears. People look in shock and in surprise. He runs up and punches me but it does nothing. I guess my Ze has gotten way stronger.

I hit him once in the stomach and he kneels down as spit flies out his mouth. I look over at Haru and Jiro.

"This is real Ze Power!", I yell as people chant and cheer. I hear one of the commentators say I look like Master Isaiah in 1987.

He charges at me again and I dodge all his punches and kicks and punch him in the face.

"Now it's my turn for my combo…G Walk!", I tell him. G Walk stands for gangster walk, an old Memphis dance I heard my mom talk about and even seen my dad do once. It used to make me laugh.

I walk towards him punching and kicking over and over and over again while moving smoothly on my feet like the dance. The crowd loses it and people run all over the bridge while yelling and recording. The officials keep them away from the fight though.

"Where did he learn that!?", I hear Master Isaiah ask.

"I don't know, but I love it!", Nia yells.

I then punch him in the air and on his way down continue the combo.

People look and cheer in amazement. I feel like Michael Jordan, or since I'm in Memphis, Ja Morant flying in the air while people cheer me on.

I finish it and he falls on the ground, bloody and defeated.

"Winner, Joseph!", the announcer calls.

People cheer and roar loudly. They chant my name and I'm actually worried that they'll break the bridge because they are so hyped.

I pick Akio up to shake his hand but he yanks his hand away.

He rises and says, "You'll pay against Haru, I promise."

"Maybe if you worried about yourself and stop relying on your cousin, you would do better.", I tell him. He frowns and I look up to see Haru staring me down.

He walks off with Haru and Jiro.

People cheer and out of nowhere, Stacy grabs my arm and holds me as if we were dating. Nia gets her off me quickly though with her hair. I'm guessing her power is some type of hair control. I wink at her saying thank you and she winks back.

As people cheer and roar I find my momma and sister in the crowd. I run to them and hug them both.

"You did it Joseph!", my mom says.

"Yea, but it's not over with yet, I still got more to do to win the whole thing.", I tell them.

Master Isaiah and Nia walks up to us.

"Glad to meet you both. I've heard great things about you.", Master Isaiah says.

"Hi, I'm Nia, Joseph's…..", Nia says then pauses.

"Girlfriend….", Savannah finishes. I pop her on her head.

"Um….", Nia says trying to word it right as her face turns red. It should be an easy no.

"It's a long story that I don't even fully know myself.", Master Isaiah tells my mom.

"Oh, ok.", my momma says in confusion.

POW! POW!

Gunshots fire and everyone scatters and run. I look through the mist of people and not to my surprise, I see No Games shooting in the air.

He sees me and directs his gun towards me.

"RUN!!!", I tell them behind me.

"JOSEPH!!", my momma and sister shouts as I run towards No Games. Nia and Master Isaiah runs behind me. No Games aims his gun towards me.

"Well if it ain't the little punk! You think just because you big shot now that you somebody and don't owe us?", he says.

Then Red Angel says, "We ain't forgot nothing, and you still a nobody!"

I look around to see people scatter in panic off the bridge. I get pissed and disappointed as I look around. This chaos, this violence, this hell, it has to end. And if no one else will end it, I will! I grab a microphone that an announcer dropped so everyone can hear me.

"Why do we always gotta do this? How come we can't ever have a goodtime without a shooting or someone always getting shot at huh?", I say in the microphone. It seems to catch them off guard. People look at me as I start to speak, so I keep it up.

"I love Memphis but do you know why I chose this bridge? This is the same bridge my father died on by a cop! Now we on live damn TV in front of the world and STILL can't act right. Someone always has to do something stupid and sadly it makes the rest of us look bad! Now you guys hate me because I made it, because I'm different, and instead of uplifting me to win and make it so I can possibly help your punk ass, you aim your gun at me, on the same bridge were my father was killed by a cop. Because of some petty beef, someone has to die huh?"

People watch from a distance and even the camera crew keeps recording. I try to hold back tears, but behind No Games and Red Angel, I can see my dad, looking at me with a smile on his face, and with thumbs up.

"Well why cowards may protect you, I won't. This nonsense violence, I won't protect it or run from it, I'll attack it back. And instead of showing the world how united we can be as black people or people in general, you aim your gun at me on the same bridge where a cop killed my dad. Well I'll be damned. Looks like as a black person I can easily die by the hands of them, and my own race. I don't even know who the enemy is anymore!", I say in anger.

People clap and chant. I've never been too hot on the race talk, but ever since my dad died I've always looked at police, and white people in general differently. But the irony of them pointing a gun at me on the same bridge where my dad died to a cop, it hits me and shows me that hate, and evil, can come from either side.

"Oh wait, yes I do. It's not the white cop, or the black gangster, it's what it's always been, and that's EVIL! And I will not stand for it or even exist with it in MY presence anymore!", I yell.

People chant and roar louder. No Games aims his gun at me again.

"JOSEPH!!!!!", I hear my momma scream.

Everything seems to move in slow motion as I think I'm living my final moments. Suddenly before he can shoot, he falls on the ground, slowly.

Behind him is Jiro. He hit him in the back of the neck knocking him out.

Haru and Akio are beside him. Red Angel tries to pick up the gun.

"I wouldn't do that if I were you my friend.", Jiro says.

Red Angel frightens up and it causes him and his gang members to run away.

Jiro stares at Master Isaiah and they both nod to each other in respect.

Nia hugs me and as soon as she lets me go, my mom and sister hugs me as well.

"I'm so proud of you!!!", my momma says as she tears up. "I know your father is so, so proud of you!"

Master Isaiah walks to me. "I told you kid. You were going to make a change."

As I open my eyes while I hug my mom, I can see my father, standing on the bridge smiling at me. He then suddenly fades away and I can't help the tears. But finally, they're tears of joy. The weight on my shoulders from my father's death has finally been released. I feel like I can finally move on now, and so can he.

But I'll never forget him.

And I know he won't forget about me.

Chapter 13. Nia's Pain

We fly to Atlanta for Nia's match the next day. Just like my match, she has an entourage of people cheering for her. She chooses her fight in front of a random house in the street.

"Why here for your fight Nia if you don't mind me asking?", I ask.

"Well this is the last place my sister lived.", she says.

"Oh, what happened?", I ask and instantly regret asking.

She looks at me as if I should know already.

"You really don't know......" She gathers herself before she cries. "This is where my sister killed herself."

As soon as she tells me that, I have some type of fantasy thought of Nia in Master Isaiah's backyard yelling and crying, and me at dinner with her and her scissor kicking me.

My head starts to shake and nod like crazy.

"Joseph? Joseph, you ok!?" She grabs me by my shoulders until I stop. "Are you ok?!", she asks in a panicked voice.

"Yea.....I am... I think.", I say in a lost, confused state.

"Joseph! My boy!"

I hear that deep fried, southern, country voice and know exactly who it is."

"Oh, hey Mr. USA.", Nia says.

He freezes, as if he stole something and got caught.

"Ohhhhhhhhhhhhhhhhhhhhhhhhhhhh…………….. Hi, Nia, how's it going.", he says in a worried voice.

"Wait, you two know each other?", I ask.

"Yea Joseph, I met him at the exhibition too. Sorry Mr. USA. He's been acting weird lately.", Nia says.

"Oh, that's strange. Well……hopefully he starts acting normal again.", Mr. USA says while sounding and acting weird.

Master Isaiah looks at Mr. USA with suspicion.

"Mr. USA…..", Master Isaiah starts.

"Yessss…. GOAT man?", he responds with caution.

"What did you do?", Master Isaiah asks.

"Whaaaaa……? I did nothing at all, what do you mean?", he says.

Master Isaiah knocks him to the ground and puts him in an arm hold that can break it.

"Now I'm going to ask again, what did you do?", Master Isaiah asks in his stern voice.

I've never seen Mr. USA like this ever.

"Fine, fine! I got Magic Moses to put a spell on him to forget Nia ever existed!", he shouts.

"You what!?", me and Nia say.

Nia then wraps her hair around his neck.

"WHY WOULD YOU DO THAT!?", she asks him while very pissed off.

"Because you broke his heart and left him lonely! He couldn't clear his head and focus on the damn tournament so I'd thought I help him out! Why are you so mad at me, you're the one who left him broken."

They let him go.

"Next time don't go meddling in people's lives if you don't know what's going on!", she shouts at him.

"So wait, I know you after all?", I ask.

"Yes dummy! We trained for five months! We both won at the exhibition! We both told each other our stories and shared our pain with each other. We kissed at the exhibition on our first date! You don't remember that?", she asks in a cracking voice.

As much as I want to lie, I can't.

"I'm sorry Nia, but I don't."

"AGHHH!" She storms off and gets ready to fight. Master Isaiah chases after her.

"Um, so we're still cool right?", Mr. USA asks me.

"Not right now Mr. USA. I have to try to remember her.", I tell him.

Time goes by and the fight gets ready.

"From Atlanta Georgia, at 5'6 weighing 135 pounds at 18 years of age, Nia! Power, hair control!"

People cheer and roar for her.

"Come on Nia!", I chant. She looks at me and looks away. I feel like she is still hurt, and so am I now.

"And from Puerto Rico, at 5'5 weighing 123 pounds at 22 years of age, Amanda! Power, Banshee Scream. Now it's Time To Scrap!"

Nia goes for a hair grab, but Amanda grabs it and pulls her to her and quickly punches her. Nia gets up and rushes her with two punches but Amanda dodges them both and screams right in Nia's face. It's so loud and it knocks Nia to the ground.

"Nia, come on this isn't your style girl!", Master Isaiah says.

"Yea you got this Nia!", I chant.

I think that distracts her more because Amanda runs over and hits her with a spin kick to Nia's face. Nia spits out blood.

She looks over at the house. I do too and remember that thought I had earlier and I have it again.

The date, the exhibition, our training. I feel my head spinning in circles like it's operating harder than it ever has.

But it hits me. The most important conversation I probably had in my life. When Nia told me about her sister and her parents. About how they pushed her to her limits. How they left her to struggle in life. And that she killed herself.

It all comes back to me the more I stare at the house. As if Nia's sister was helping me in a weird way.

Nia gets kicked again and struggles to get up.

"NIA!!! I remember!!", I shout.

People look at me like a crazy person.

"I remember our date! I remember our kiss! Our training. I remember you are the first person I threw a Ze blast at. I remember why you're even here. Your sister! You want to do this for her and prove your parents you don't need them! I know she's gone but it's not too late to do it for her! Get up now Nia!!!"

She stumbles to her feet and her hometown cheers her on. She looks at me and I see the fire in her eyes again. They look like how they did when she saved me from No Games and Red Angel, when she trained with me, when she got mad at me when I flipped her, and when she was angry and beat Carlos.

It was at that moment; I knew she won.

She charges at Amanda but Amanda yells again, knocking her back to the ground, but she gets up. The commentators hype up the fight.

Amanda makes a big mistake and goes for another spinning kick, but Nia grabs her midair and slams her to the ground.

"Yes Nia!", me, Master Isaiah, and Mr. USA chant.

As Amanda gets back up she readies up for another yell, but Nia wraps her hair around her mouth. Then she picks her up with her hair and tosses her across the street onto a car. The windows shatter and people roar in excitement. As Amanda gets up, Nia whips her with her hair and sweeps her from her feet. Amanda falls and doesn't get up.

"Winner, Nia!" the announcer calls.

Everyone chants her name. She jumps up and down in happiness. Her friends and city surround her and lift her up.

When they put her down, Master Isaiah walks up to her and congratulates her. She and Amanda shake hands. Amanda cries though. She tells Nia she needed the money to survive. She doesn't have help and no one will help her and she has no family. Nia makes a promise that she'll win and help her and they both hug and cry.

I approach Nia and put my hand out for her to shake it.

"Good job.", I say.

"Are you kidding me? A handshake?", she says as tears fall from her eyes.

"What?", I respond in confusion.

She rushes towards me and kisses me like she hasn't seen me in 10 years.

"I love you.", she says.

"I love you too.", I say.

We kiss again and tears flow from her eyes.

"So why did you offer that weak ass handshake?", she asks and smiles.

"Girl I forgot you existed for a minute; I couldn't just jump in with a kiss."

We both smile and laugh.

"Finally! Are you two back to normal!?", Master Isaiah asks us in relief.

We both laugh and say yes.

"Good! Now that both of you are passed your depressed stage, you can actually focus."

"Maybe we can find you someone special Master Isaiah?", Nia mocks.

"Don't play with me, I'll kick both of your asses!", he says.

We both laugh.

"Also, I'm sorry for saying you're not important to me.", she says.

"It's fine, I'm sorry for agreeing to forget about you."

Two adults walk up to us and Nia gets out of my arms.

"Mom, dad, please no.", Nia begs.

"We just wanted to say good job and that we're proud of you.", her dad says.

"No! Please, just go.", Nia says.

"Fine, but just remember, we're the reason you're here. You wouldn't be here if it wasn't for us.", her mother says.

"Hey…", I say stepping in.

"No Joseph, it's ok. This is what they do. Make every situation about them. This is their specialty. Don't be surprised. Just like you told me it was my fault Nivea killed herself and that she was always weak huh?", Nia says with a lot of power in her voice, but not loudly.

The mom snickers and they walk off.

"You have asshole parents. I'm sorry I had to say it.", Mr. USA says.

"No it's fine, it's actually satisfying hearing someone else say it and not just me. Also, sorry for choking you earlier.", she tells Mr. USA.

"Ah, that's water under the bridge. Also sorry for making things messy. That's not what America is about.", he says putting his hand in a salute position over his head.

"Speaking of water, how did your match go Mr. USA?", I ask.

"What type of question is that. I won kid so I could kick your ass! He was tougher than I thought, but what is water to muscle.", he says then laughs out loud

"Ok, just have to tell my old co-workers about this.", I say smirking.

Mr. USA walks away and Me and Nia walk together down the street hand in hand. We just talk and catch up with each other and I really enjoy her company. Even though she's my girl, she's also my best friend. A girl walks towards us with a baby in her hand.

"Nia I heard you won! Congratulations girl!", the girl says.

"Thank you Regan!", Nia says.

They hug each other. She hands the baby over to Nia.

"Joseph, meet Naya, my sister's daughter.", she tells me.

I look at the baby and she gives a cute smile at me and I smile at her.

"Here, hold her, she's only 2 months old so hold her carefully.", Nia says.

"You sure? I've never held a baby before, I don't want to….", I say as Nia interrupts me.

"Joseph hold my niece.", she demands.

She puts the baby in my hands and I hold her with care. She spits on me a little and laughs. It irritates me but her laugh makes me laugh too.

"I have to watch her now and while I'm gone, I let my cousin Regan watch her."

"Hey, nice to meet you Regan I'm…", I say as she cuts me off.

"Oh I know who you are. You're that boy from Memphis who gave that speech. It's trending. Nice to meet you."

"Really, it is?", I say.

"Yea, plus when Nia came home she kept talking about how she misses you and how she messed up and…."

"Okay! That's enough catching up!", Nia Interrupts.

She gets Naya out my hand and gives her to Regan. She tells them to go to the house and she'll meet up with them later.

"So, I'm guessing you're staying here for now huh?", I ask.

"Yea, I have to help watch Naya. Plus my aunt and family are grieving for my sister so I need to be here. I really wish I could go back to Memphis with you and Master Isaiah like it used to be but…", she says. I stop her.

"No, it's fine. I promise I understand. You just make sure I see you again fighting, and you better not lose.", I tell her.

"Um-hm. I should be telling you that.", she says.

 I kiss her again and she waves goodbye and we both go home.

Chapter 14. The Rematch

I go back home to Memphis and Regan was right. I'm trending and I'm like a superhero in my city now. I don't know if it's because the fight, the speech, or both. To be honest, I don't know where the speech came from. I guess I was just fed up. It was my dad. He was with me and guided me through the speech. Just like I feel like Nia's sister help me remember who Nia was. It's crazy.

I visit my mom and sister a couple times to make sure there're good, but I still stay with Master Isaiah to train. My mom is still unable to work right now, but the community is taking real good care of her right now. Everyone is making sure they are good, so I am good to fight. I have all of Memphis in my corner, plus God.

My next fight is tomorrow. I fight a girl named Irina from Russia. At least I'm not afraid to fight a girl now, thanks to Nia. I do some research on her to try to get an advantage.

I find out she doesn't have a power in particular. She's very advance in hand combat though. Some even say she's the best hand fighter in the world, man or woman. But she does have an ability that is very critical to my fighting style. The more damage she takes, the stronger she gets. People have described her getting so hurt in a fight, but so strong that her punches end up feeling like trains running into your face. If she knows about me, which she probably does, she'll probably let me hurt her real bad so she can hit me with one hit. I'll have to look out for it. I train with Master Isaiah a little more, meditate, then heal and relax my body and get ready to head to Russia tomorrow.

We wake up and board our flight and head to Russia. The fight is located at Mount Elbrus. As we arrive, people show up. It's not as crowded as me or Nia's fight though. It could be because we're in the mountains, or because Mr. USA fights Mr. Russia at St. Basil's Cathedral today. That's the main fight that most people want to see today. Even people from America come over to watch that fight, but Irina has a decent size crowd as well.

I finally see her and she is huge!

"From Kazan Russia, at 6'4 and 181 pounds at 23 years of age, Irina! Power, the ability to get stronger as she fights!"

People cheer and roar for her and chant Russia. They also mock me and call me American boy, but I try not to get dragged into the USA and Russian 2pac and Biggie beef.

"And from Memphis Tennessee, at 6'0 weighing 174 pounds at 18 years of age, Joseph! Power, Ze Power!"

They boo me so loudly that it feels like Amanda is yelling directly in my ear.

"Time to Scrap!!", the announcer yells.

Irina and I circle around each other.

"Listen here boy, I can care less about the American and Russian beef. I'm just here to beat you and I'm not going to lose!", she says to me over the roar of people throughout the mountains.

"Same, but sorry I'm winning this!", I tell her with confidence.

She throws a leg sweep, but I flip over it. She then rushes me with a combo of punches. I dodge all of them and catch the last one and stare at her.

She catches me off guard and then head buds me hard in the face. I stumble back and she gives me no time to recover and kicks me dead on the side of my face, knocking me on the ground.

People chant and roar but somehow through all that I hear Master Isaiah yelling, telling me to get up. As I rise to my feet again, she rushes towards me.

"Ze Blast!!!", I yell as I throw a Ze blast. It hits her and knocks her down.

Now, people boo me and chant for her to get up. Then it instantly hits me that she's now probably way stronger than before, and that kick hit hard as hell already.

I spit out blood and charge another attack to try to finish her off and it hits her again. But to my disappointment, she gets up. The look in her face tells me that I messed up with her grinning, and I may have.

She pops her neck and rushes towards me, this time way faster, and she punches me directly in my stomach. I fly all the way back through some trees, even breaking most of them. It's easily the most pain I've felt from a single punch in my life and even with my Ze activated, it hurts like hell.

People cheer and roar and I hear the announcer counting for me to get back in the fighting area.

"Joseph, come on!!!", I hear Master Isaiah yell.

I struggle to get on my feet and walk back to the area as the announcer counts down.

"I…..can't lose…now!", I tell myself as I walk back.

As soon as the announcer says one, I enter the area. My arms are bloody and so is my whole body. Irina gets an impressed look on her face.

"Hm, you got up. Respect.", she says.

"I'm…not….losing.", I struggle to say.

"Oh you already have.", she responds.

She rushes towards me again but this time I get low and catch her leg with my legs and I flip her. She falls face first. As she rises I hit her with a scissor kick. The crowd looks in awe as their fighter lies on the ground. My Ze is activated so every move I make does even more damage.

She rises and yells and tries to combo me. I dodge them but I feel the wind from her punches due to how fast and strong she's swinging. I try to hit her after she misses one of her punches, but she backflips and kicks me in the air as she does so.

Blood shoots out my mouth.

"This is getting too close!", I hear Master Isaiah yell.

"Yea it is, I'll end it for you!", Irina shouts.

She jumps high in the air to me. She kicked me at least 30 feet in the air and I'm still going up as she jumps up to me.

"It's over kid!", she says.

But she messed up.

"Oh yea, let's see!", I say.

I grab her leg and tighten my body to get stronger from the Ze. I then spin around and throw her to the ground as hard as I can. It creates a crater in the ground due to the hard impact. She tries her hardest to get up but she doesn't.

"Winner, Joseph!", the announcer calls.

The crowd boo's me, but I walk over to Irina and give her my hand to help her up. She takes it and put's my arm in the air and shows good sportsmanship to the crowd.

Then suddenly with all she has, plus the power she already had gained from the fight, she knees me in the stomach so hard that even she falls afterwards. People cheer as I cough out blood. Master Isaiah and the tournament officials runs over to me to help me and to the crowd to try to calm them down.

They put Irina in cuffs but she tells me something as she's being arrested.

"Remember, I beat myself! You never beat me you weaker punk!" I lie on my back trying to breathe again.

They take her away and Master Isaiah guides me through the hostile crowd. We go to our hotel and decide to leave first thing tomorrow as soon as possible.

"That was crazy!", I say as I sit on the couch still trying to recover.

"Yea, but I've seen worse. I've seen people die after fights because they lost. Hell, if someone catches us in the streets, they might shoot us.", Master Isaiah says.

"Damn! This tournament is serious huh?", I ask.

"Very.", he tells me.

I look on my phone to see who's all left in the tournament.

Joseph

Chen

Haru

Nia

Mr. Russia

Polar Zero

Kaya

I notice that I don't see someone that I should.

"Yo! Mr. USA lost!", I say in disbelief with my eyes wide open.

"Really?", Master Isaiah says.

"Yea, that's crazy. Also sad, I know he was really looking forward for our rematch."

"Well, he may not get his rematch, but Haru will if he beats Chen. And he's going to be way harder than Akio and Irina. You're going to have to step up your game if you want to win.", he tells me.

"Yessir.", I respond.

I remember the commentators saying how good Chen is. If Haru beats him today, then I'll know he'll be way tougher than he was at the exhibition.

We fly back to Memphis the next morning. People congratulate me and have a block party for me. I don't stay for long though. My ribs still hurt from Irina kneeing me and I still need to recover my body.

I have to fly out to Japan tomorrow. But Nia has a match today in South Africa against Kaya. I call her to wish her good luck. I remember how good of a fighter Kaya was at the exhibition so I know that it'll be tough, even for Nia. She seemed surprised and happy when she heard my voice and I was too when I heard hers. She sounded determined and promised that she'll win.

When I got off the phone, something hits me. What if me and Nia have to fight each other? That'll probably be the best fight that can happen, even more than Mr. USA vs Mr. Russia. Both of us trained by the first tournament winner Master Isaiah, with tragic backstories, and will our relationship change if one of us beats the other? I try not to think about it no more and think about Haru. That's all that matters right now. I know he's starving for a rematch and I'll have to match his energy if I want to win.

When the fight for Nia vs Kaya happens, me and Master Isaiah watch it in his living room as soon as I hopped out the bath. Kaya has a huge fan following and Magic Moses is there too to support Kaya. I wish I was there for Nia.

As the fight starts, Kaya yells and tries to stab Nia with one of her long spears.

"Is that allowed? She can kill her!", I say to Master Isaiah.

"Kaya has been trained to not kill, and if an accident were to happen, the tournament isn't held responsible.", he tells me.

"I don't remember that when I signed up.", I tell him.

"It comes with the territory kid. People are fighting with powers, accidents are expected.", he tells me.

Nia dodges the rapid spear attacks, but Kaya's speed and intensity is unlike anything I've seen. Nia gets overwhelmed and eventually gets stabbed in her thigh. She lets out a large scream in pain and Master Isaiah and I cringe as we watch.

Nia gets pissed and as Kaya goes for another attack, Nia takes one of her spears with her hair. She then runs towards Kaya, but Kaya with her other spear jumps on her spear and balance on it with the sharp side on the ground.

Everyone, including me and Master Isaiah and the commentators, watch in awe as she somehow balances on the skinny, long spear, getting out of Nia's way.

Nia is also shocked, but as soon as she tries to kick the spear, Kaya drop kicks her in the face, knocking Nia down. With her bad leg, she tries to get up, but falls back down.

"Come on Nia!", I chant threw the TV as me and Master Isaiah watch on our feet now.

Nia somehow gets to her feet at the last second. Kaya then stabs Nia in her shoulder and Nia lets out another yell in pain, but she doesn't fall. She quickly whips Kaya in her face with her hair in a quick reaction and it knocks Kaya down.

Kaya gets up and throws her spear at Nia, but Nia ducks under it. Now Kaya's spears are out of her hand. Nia runs towards Kaya, but Kaya surprises Nia with her impressive hand to hand combat skills. Kaya punches and kicks Nia a lot.

Nia stumbles back a little and spits blood. But as soon as Kaya jumps to kick Nia again, Nia catches her with her hair and slams her hard to the ground. The thud can even be heard threw the TV.

Me and Master Isaiah get hyped, but Nia falls down as blood leaks from her leg and shoulder.

"Wait, what happens if they both get knocked out? Is there a rematch?", I ask Master Isaiah.

"No, both are just eliminated from the tournament", he tells me.

"What! Why?", I ask.

"Because the first fight as you can see is already damaging enough. If both of them can't get up, then how are they going to fight again without one of them, or maybe even both of them dying.", he explains.

It makes sense because they won't have enough time to recover fast enough to fit the tournament's schedule. We both chant for Nia to get up, but all of South Africa chants for Kaya.

With only three seconds left, I see Nia's arm twitch. And she somehow gets enough life to get up within three seconds. Nia wins her match and me and Master Isaiah clap in happiness, like our team won the Superbowl.

The fight gets off air, but I know how dangerous it could be if a fighter beats the other one in their hometown from my personal experience with Irina. I try not to worry about it too much and I relax on my phone.

Later that night, I find out that they are both trending under "#blacksisterlove" because they both hugged and cried after the match. Apparently Kaya needed the money to afford care for people in her village dying from a disease. Nia promised to help her when she won just like she did for Amanda. Someone recorded the whole thing and it was very wholesome to watch as people clapped. I wish any of my fights ended like this. So far all my fights end with gunshots, or someone being arrested. I'm glad Nia is promising to help people, but I'm winning this tournament.

I also find out that Haru won in his fight against Chen. I see pictures of them both bloody, but with Haru with his arms in the air. I know that I'll have to win quickly during our fight, but I get excited, as I can't wait to fight him. He has to fight back-to-back days, so I'll try to use that to my advantage.

We fly out to Tokyo the next morning and all the traveling is starting to hit me and Master Isaiah. We go out to eat some food but take it back to our hotel. Apparently, Japan hates me because I beat Haru and Akio, and they definitely already hate Master Isaiah because of his past with Jiro. We leave and go to Jiro's dojo. Haru doesn't choose anywhere fancy to fight and it kind of works to his advantage. It's where he trains and that's like me or Nia fighting someone in Master Isaiah's backyard. Nia gives me a call and wishes me good luck.

The dojo is pretty big but is crowded full of people. It's easily the most crowded fight I've seen and been to in my life. There's at least 2,000 people inside and more thousands outside watching from a monitor and the streets. I heard people have been camping here for over three days to have a seat. I even hear the commentator say this is the most people in attendance ever recorded to see a Time to Scrap fight that wasn't for the championship.

"The history of this fight goes all the way back to Isaiah vs Jiro! The next gen fight! Who will come out victorious in this epic rematch!", the commentator yells over the roar and sea of people.

As I tie my shoes I hear a deep fried, southern, grown in the field, sunflower seeds, deep American voice. It's Mr. USA.

"This place is dumped! Even more than my match.", he says.

"Yea, I'm surprised to see you here. I'm sorry for your match.", I say.

"Ah, it's nothing. Me and him are exactly the same. He just got the better of me and he had home advantage. But I'm not here for me kid. I'm in your corner and supporting you the whole fight and the whole tournament.", he tells me.

"Thanks Mr. USA, it means a lot.", I tell him.

He then slaps me hard in my face.

"What the hell is wrong with you!", I say in anger.

"That was to get you fired up kid! Now, go out there and win!!!"

I grin and walk to Haru who's in the middle of the mat.

"From Tokyo Japan, at 6'2 weighing 181 pounds at 20 years of age, Haru! Power, Ze Power!", the announcer yells.

People chant and roar Haru that it's loud to even hear the announcer yell my name.

"From Memphis, Tennessee…"

As soon as he says Tennessee, the crowd boo's me so loud it's hard to hear the rest.

"At 6'0 weighing 174 pounds at 18 years of age, Joseph!"

The boo's get louder.

"Power, Ze power!"

Me and Haru get even closer to each other staring each other down, both of us knowing what's on the line.

"Time to Scrap!!!"

Chapter 15. Joseph VS Haru!

As soon as the announcer says scrap, Haru yells and goes for a direct punch towards my face, but I dodge it. He goes for another one and I dodge it and I try to sweep him off his feet, but he jumps over it. He then flips and tries to kick me, but I somersault backwards out the way. He then tries a series of combos and I duck all of them and then catch his last punch. I go for a head bud, but he twists my arm and flips me on the ground. He tries to kick me in the eye, but I hurry and roll out the way. We both get into our stance as the crowd roars.

Neither one of us with an advantage. I go for my G Walk combo, but he dodges all my punches.

"You want to fight for real now?", he asks.

"Hm, it'll be a good change in pace, plus I'm done with the warmup.", I say back.

"Good.", he says.

He gets into his stance and so do I. He swings and goes for a right punch, and I dodge it, but I don't pay attention to his left and he hits me with a small Ze blast to the right side of my face. I fall to the ground.

"Joseph!!", I hear Mr. USA scream.

Haru then jumps on me and holds me down as he keeps punching me. The crowd is going crazy screaming at me to give up.

"Get up son!!!", Master Isaiah yells.

All of Haru punches are with his Ze power and I try to protect myself with my Ze, but I still feel the pain and his Ze power. It's somehow way stronger than it was at the exhibition. I yell as I try to get Ze power, and I blast him in his chest. He falls back. We both get up and he chuckles as my face is bloodier than it has ever been.

I try to catch my breath. I tighten my body and my Ze appears around my body.

"You'll pay for that.", I say in a normal but stern voice.

"Hmph, we'll see about that.", he says.

"Oh that wasn't a suggestion, that was a promise.", I tell him.

Master Isaiah looks at me with a grin on his face. That must have made Haru upset, because he charges at me with another Ze punch. I matrix duck under it, but I go all the way back to where my arms are touching the ground. He's close enough so I kick him with one foot up his chin. He falls back and I blast him with a Ze blast.

The crowd boo's me and chant for Haru to rise to his feet.

He does.

Then me and him both yell as we throw a Ze blast at each other, but it explodes. So, we throw another one and it does the same thing. Then we rush into each other and do what I can only describe as pure scrapping.

Both of us sending hits and taking hard ones. Then we both hit each other at the same time as hard as we possibly can. It feels like my head was just squashed by a hammer, but I squashed his as well.

The world seems to move in slow motion after the impact. We both fall, and the announcer begins to count down from ten. We both struggle to get on our feet and the crowd chants for Haru to get up.

He gets up at five while I still stumble. I hear Master Isaiah and Mr. USA yelling for me to get up.

I barely get to my feet at two.

The crowd, I think, cheer in respect of this fight. Haru grins at me and I grin back as we get back in our stance. I can hear my mom and sister yelling at the TV in my head. I can feel Nia encouraging me and pushing me to win. I can hear my boss, co-workers, Jamal, and everyone else in Memphis yelling for me to win. I can feel my father looking down on me, telling me I can do it.

I close my eyes and take a deep breath.

I hear Haru yelling, and he runs towards me. I open my eyes to see his body dosed in white smoke and glow. I do the same when I open my eyes and jump over him. I then quickly turn around and charge a giant Ze blast.

"I told you….", I say as he turns around.

The crowd gasp, as the blast gets bigger.

"I PROMISE!!!", I yell as I throw the blast.

"HARU!!!", Jiro yells.

The blast hits him and it's so big it blinds everyone inside.

"It must be over! It has to be over!", I hear the commentator yell in excitement.

I see Haru laid out flat on his back. I smile, but it's short lived.

Haru somehow, someway, gains enough energy to get on his feet when the announcer counts down to three.

The crowd loses it.

"FINISH THE JOB JOSEPH!!!", Master Isaiah yells.

I rush over to him yelling to punch him before he can fully recover, but when I do, he grabs my face and blasts me with Ze in the face. It feels like my face was on fire. I bend over to gather myself, but I feel him axe kick me in the back of my head. I fall face first to the ground and the crowd cheers and roars.

The announcers calls the match as I lie on the ground in a bloody puddle. People chant and roar.

"THIS IS TOO MUCH! I'M ENDING IT NOW!", the announcers says.

"Kid…", I hear Mr. USA say.

"I told you Isaiah, Haru doesn't lose!", Jiro tells Master Isaiah as I lie on the ground unconscious.

"I……. I can't…….I won't…….", I say to myself in my head.

GET UP SON! GET UP NOW AND USE ALL OF YOUR FAITH!

I hear a voice, sounding like my father, telling me to get up.

"NO!" I yell.

The whole building freezes.

"Excuse me?", the announcer says.

I somehow, someway, get on my feet.

"I said…. NOOOOO!!!", I yell.

I let out a Ze wave knocking over the crowd and Haru.

"This match isn't over yet!", I say sternly as my white aura gets bigger and stronger.

"So you don't know when to quit huh? Fine, I'll make you!!!", Haru yells. As he does, his aura gets stronger too. It sounds like a dragon roar yelled instead of him, but I'm not intimidated by it.

He runs to me and punches me hard as hell in the face. It spins me around a little, but I turn around back punching him in the face even harder. It spins him around. I then send 15 small Ze blast to his back and then I drop kick him to the ground.

"This is the best match of all time!!!", I hear the announcer yell as the crowd goes crazy. "These two want it and damn it they want it bad!!! Who wants it more!? Is it Joseph or is it Haru!!!", he screams.

I struggle to stand on my feet and blood is rushing from my head down my body. He gets up and tries to punch me, but I grab his fist and knee him in his stomach.

In anger, he gets up and knees me back. We both stand holding our stomachs trying to gather our breath.

"I'll die before you beat me again!", he says.

"Well you might want to just die because I'm not losing!", I yell back.

Then we both think the same exact thing.

ZE……..", he starts to yell.

POWER!!!!!", I finish.

We both charge the biggest Ze blasts we could possibly gather and throw it. It explodes and throws us both back. We both lie on the ground and the count begins. I can hear Haru yelling in pain, and I do too. The count gets to seven. The crowd chants for Haru to rise. I can hear Master Isaiah and Mr. USA telling me to get up.

"Six!"

No one is still up. The crowd gets rowdier.

"Five!"

Nothing

"Four!"

Nothing

"Three!"

We both start to stumble to get up. I rise more than Haru though.

"Two!"

"COME ON JOSEPH!!!!!", Master Isaiah yells.

"One!"

As we stumble, Haru rises all the way.

"AGHH!", I yell as my body gives up on me…

…and I fall back to the ground.

"IT'S OVER!!! IT'S ALL OVER!!! HARU! HARU! HARU!!!!!!", I hear the announcer yell.

The crowd erupts and some even rush to put Haru in the air like Atlanta did Nia.

I lie on the ground in the worst pain I've ever felt in my life.

I failed…

I failed…

I…. lost.

Chapter 16. The Politics of the Tournament

As the security and officials clear the mat, I hear Haru calling, searching for me. To my surprise, he rushes over to me before Master Isaiah and Mr. USA can. He sticks his hand out to help me to my feet. I reach my hand out, but as soon as I do, he pulls his hand away. I look at him in shock.

"I promise, you'll fail, my friend.", he says.

He walks away and leaves me on the ground.

Master Isaiah and Mr. USA rush over to me to help me.

The crowd chants Haru, and Jiro. They also chant Japan. Master Isaiah carries me out of the dojo. I cry as he carries me, in pain, and in disappointment. We finally exit the dojo.

"Where's Mr. USA?", I ask as I cry.

"I don't know, but we need to get out of here before it gets too crazy!", he says.

We go back to the hotel but as we enter the car, I fall asleep.

I wake up on the couch. It feels like it was all a dream. I really wish it was.

I wish I could pack up my fighting clothes and enter the dojo as if nothing ever happened and act like that was just a practice fight. But as the pain starts to hit me again, I remember that it was all very real.

I try to ignore it, but I look at my phone to see Nia has called me 50 times. My mom has called me 20 times. And I'm trending, but I know it's not because I won.

Master Isaiah walks towards me.

"So you finally woke up? Bout time."

I just stare at him and can't stop the tears from flowing down my face. He sits on the couch beside me.

"Why the hell are you crying?", he asks as if he's not aware.

"Why do you think!? I lost! I failed! You told me on day one to not disappoint you and waste your time. I wasted everybody's time! All of this was for nothing! I can't help my mother! My sister! My damn self!", I cry in anger and sadness.

"Your city is taking care of your mother son.", Master Isaiah says.

"THAT'S NOTHING! They did the same thing when my father died! And just like they did him, when they forget about me, no one will help us! You can't depend on other people for your problems!", I cry.

He slaps me.

I look at him in shock.

"Enough! You've depended on people your whole journey kid! I don't know if you notice, but I've helped you, Nia helped you, your whole city plus your family supported you, plus the world and the black community. I don't know if you pay attention to the news, but that speech you gave hit hard and was a wakeup call to many black people and people in general out there! YOU told them the war was on good and evil, not black and white. And most importantly your father and God helped you. If you think you did all this by yourself, you're crazy! You try to act independent and that's fine, but there is NEVER anything wrong with help as long as it's genuine help, which it has! You've made the most impactful debut in The Time to Scrap Tournament EVER! No one has made as much progress in five months ever. It's almost impossible to even think how far you've come. You need to be at peace with that. But don't ever forget this hurt, remember it and come back in four more years and win!"

A long pause of quietness fills the room.

"Don't make the same mistake as me Joseph. Don't let one lost define who you are. In a fight, or life. You learn from your mistakes and come back stronger with your head up high, you hear me?", Master Isaiah says.

I nod my head yeah.

I sit on the couch and open my phone. I scroll through my feed, and I see a video of a street fight uploaded with the hashtag Time to Scrap. In the video someone says beat his ass like Joseph. It makes me smile for half a second only. Maybe I have left an incredible impact on the Time to Scrap Tournament after all.

Master Isaiah turns on the TV, but all the people reporting the fight were speaking in Japanese, so we couldn't understand.

We hear a knock on the door and Master Isaiah asks who it is.

In his deep fried, southern biscuit style, goats on the field, straw hat wearing, football loving voice, Mr. USA says it's him.

He rushes through the door and shuts it fast, like he's hiding from someone.

"Hey kid, sorry for your lost.", he says.

"It's fine.", I desperately say lying to myself wiping my tears.

"Isaiah, I think you should know this.", he says. Mr. USA is usually a loud, goofy man but he sounds very, very serious.

Master Isaiah picks up on this tone as well.

"What is it?", he asks concerningly.

"I debated even telling you this, but you deserve to know the truth. Jiro…. he's been using….Khaos for his fighters. Most importantly, Akio and Haru.", Mr. USA says.

"Look I understand you're upset because you both lost, but we just have to deal with the fact that America took an L, unless Nia wins.", Master Isaiah says.

"This is FACT Isaiah! Look, I'll take my L and move on, I promise I will. But that boy over there…" He points to me. "He wasn't supposed to lose that fight. I caught them with my own eyes. You guys left before me. I caught Akio leaving and a clear needle fell out his backpack. I promise. It was filled with a black substance, which me and you both know is the Khaos drug."

"What's that?", I ask.

"Khaos is a drug that works like steroids, but for your genetics. It can make you taller, stronger, and enhance people's power. You know powers are genetically passed, but even if your power isn't passed down, like Ze, it can still enhance it.", he says.

I snap. "So…. they cheated! Both of them!", I say in anger.

"Well…no.", Mr. USA says.

"What do you mean no!", I say.

"While it's heavily looked down on, Khaos isn't illegal in the tournament. They even let people with no powers to use it to somewhat compete in the tournament. But if someone with powers uses it, it's looked at as a scum move. It was a long debate back in the day, but they eventually agreed that if people with no powers can use it, so can people with them. And I wonder….", Mr. USA pauses.

Master Isaiah fills in the blanks. "Jiro used that to beat me when they stole Ze. I was right all this time!"

He slams his fist on the coffee table.

"What do we do then?", I ask.

"We must report this!", Mr. USA says. "This is disgraceful! Yea it's not cheating, but where's the honor!?"

"That's not going to change anything Mr. USA. We both know that. They didn't break any rules. And plus, Time to Scrap has never been about honor.", Master Isaiah says. "We…. we just have to move on."

"No!", I say. They both look at me. "We'll deal with it with the officials after the tournament, but for now we need to warn Nia. She still has a chance at winning. We have to warn her.", I tell them.

They both nod their heads.

The next morning we head to our flights back to Memphis. Mr. USA comes with us instead of going back to Dallas. I look on my phone to see that Mr. Russia and Polar Zero ended in a draw, eliminating them both, leaving the last match to be Nia vs Haru.

We land in Memphis and instead of going to Master Isaiah's house, I go to my house. But word gets out that I'm home and people cheer for me. They congratulate me and cheer for me even though I lost. Jax, Jamal, my co-workers, even some of the gang members that hang with No Games and Red Angel congratulate me.

When I can finally get to my house, I feel a relieving feeling. I haven't been home in forever and it feels good to be back. My sister and mom run to me in the living room and hug me full of tears.

"I'm so sorry baby. We watched the whole thing, and you gave it your all.", my momma says.

"It's ok momma, but I have to leave.", I say.

Why? Where are you going now?", she asks.

"I have to go help Nia, she needs my help and I have to go to Atlanta now to warn her and be at her fight for support."

"Warn her of what?", Savannah asks.

"There's some scandalous stuff going on in the background. It's how I lost.", I tell them.

"What? They cheated?", my momma asks.

"Technically no, but if I don't tell Nia, she won't have a fair chance. Master Isaiah and Mr. USA are going with me. I have to go now.", I tell them in a hurry.

"Ok son, you can go. But please don't come back bloody again."

"Yes ma'am.", I say.

I walk out the door and Master Isaiah and Mr. USA wait for me in Mr. USA's nice car. We don't have money for a flight, and the tournament isn't funding our flights anymore. Mr. USA has money, but enough to get all of us onboard a plane, plus he lost so America isn't going to fund him.

It's about a six-hour drive from Memphis to Atlanta, so we have no time to lose. As soon as I get in we take off for the interstate.

Chapter 17. For You!

It takes us forever to get there. I keep trying to call Nia, but she doesn't answer her phone. We eventually get to Atlanta and I lead them directly to Nia's sister's old house. Nobody is there.

"This is where I last saw her.", I say.

"Her dead…sisters house. This is where you thought she'll be and lived at?", Master Isaiah asks.

"I mean….where else can we go?", I ask.

"Anywhere but here! Who lives in a house where their sibling died in Joseph!", Mr. USA says.

"You got any bright ideas Mr. real American.", I mock in frustration.

"Not right now but when I do it'll be better than your dumbass one.", he says.

"Hey! Enough.", Master Isaiah says. "Arguing will do nothing……………..but this was a dumb place to start Joseph."

"Well sorry that I had faith Master!", I say.

"Yea, dumb faith.", Mr. USA says.

I get irritated at them both and hop out the car.

I call Nia as I pace back in forth on the sidewalk, but still no answer. I throw a rock in a stream of water on the other side of the road in anger. I sit on the sidewalk with my face down.

Someone calls my name.

"What you doing down here legend?"

I look up and it's Regan, pushing Naya with a stroller.

"Oh yes! I'm looking for Nia, do you know where she is?", I ask with hope.

"Oh she's already left. I thought you would know that seeing you two are tighter than a stuck shoe knot."

"Who talks like tha…never mind, so they already left?", I ask in confusion.

"Yep. That Haru guy wanted to fight as soon as possible, so they moved their fight to today.", she explains.

"Damn it! Ok thanks. Bye-bye.", I say.

Before I enter the car I hear Naya making baby noises.

"Bye-bye Naya. I have to go help your auntie."

I hop in the car and tell them that Nia has already left.

"Where is the championship fight being held?", I ask them.

"The same country the exhibition was in, America.", Mr. USA says "But it's in New York since the exhibition was in California.", he finishes.

"New York? How are we getting there?", I ask.

"I don't know, but gas is too tight for that and I don't have enough cash to make it there at the moment. That wasn't in the budget.", Mr. USA says.

"How does America's number one fighter not have money falling out of his pockets?!", I ask.

"Son, it's not about the money, plus I give that back to America and give it away to charity. Plus plus, the money I do get is invested, I'm not stupid. I do know about generational wealth. And even if I got the money, we wouldn't make it to New York in time.", he tells me.

"I'm sorry Joseph, but we're short on options right now.", Master Isaiah says.

"There's gotta be a way!", I say in desperation.

A moment of silence fills the car.

"UGHHHHH!!!! FINE! Get out the car.", Mr. USA says.

"What is it?", Master Isaiah asks.

"Get out and you'll see.", Mr. USA responds.

We get out the car and get on the sidewalk.

"Now I usually don't partake in illegal mess but I will this one time. Don't tell nobody though, I got an American reputation to keep up with.", he tells us.

"What are you finna do?', I ask.

He grabs me and Master Isaiah on the side of him and jumps so high and far in the air I nearly pee myself.

"WHAT THE HELL ARE YOU DOING?!!", I ask.

"THIS IS CRAZY!!!", Master Isaiah yells.

"You need to get to New York, so I'm going to get you to New York. Try to be less loud though, I can't get caught using my powers!", he says.

We literally jump through cities and states in minutes. I knew he was strong, but this is ridiculous. Me and Master Isaiah try not to scream, but we fail. It's like the scariest roller coaster ride ever. He misjudges a jump and we end up in a deep lake.

"Oops, sorry about that", he says as we jump out the lake.

He jumps so high that we get eye level with airplanes and can see kids and adults pointing at us in amazement.

We eventually land in New York city and head to the arena building. Mr. USA stops though.

"What are you doing, come on!", I say.

"You two keep going, I'm going back to get my car."

"What? Come on this is important!", I tell him.

"So is my Bentley fool! I did my part, now go do yours….GOAT man.", he tells me. He smiles at me and I smile back. He jumps away into the night sky and Master Isaiah and I rush in the fight.

Security tried to stop us but they realize who I am and they let us in.

"Feels good huh?", Master Isaiah says.

"Yes it does.", I respond.

We continue rushing and go to the back to find Nia, but we don't see her. We search all through the halls of the arena, but don't find her.

"Where could she be, she has to be here.", I say.

Then suddenly me and Master Isaiah are being hung upside down by our feet. We hear a big burst of laughter behind us.

"You two look stupid!!", Nia laughs.

"Put us down Nia, now is not the time for games!", Master Isaiah says.

"You're right. It's TIME TO SCRAP!", she yells in excitement and happiness. She keeps laughing. I can tell she's so happy to be in the final fight.

"No seriously Nia, put us down!", I say trying to convince her that we're not playing right now.

"Oh yea, you're right." She puts us down and hugs me.

"I'm so sorry Joseph. I watched the whole thing and you gave it your all." She keeps trying to kiss me and I keep removing my head trying to explain the situation.

"Yea…yea…I'm fine now…..I promise…..but you need to listen to me now."

She stops

"What's wrong?", she asks.

"Haru is using Khaos, a power enhancer that Master Isaiah said he thought Jiro used. That's how he beat me.", I tell her.

"What!? Really!?", she says surprised.

"Yes.", Master Isaiah says.

"Then, then how the hell am I going to win?", Nia asks stressing out. I grab her arms.

"Listen to me Nia, my faith and determination was so strong, that I didn't even know he was cheating until after the fight. That means even with his Khaos, he still struggled against me, and you're better than me, you've always have been.", I say.

"But…", she interrupts.

"No buts. You can do this. Had I known he was cheating, I would've won. But now you do know. Now go win.", I tell her like a coach talking to their players.

"Ok, Joseph."

We walk to the fighting mat and the crowd goes crazy. I even hear some chants for me and Master Isaiah. Before the announcer starts, Nia tells me something.

"Joseph, I've been fighting the tournament for me and everyone else. But this one…..is for you."

When I heard that…I knew with 100% certainty…..that Nia was going to win it all.

IT'S THE TIME YOU'VE BEEN WAITING FOR...

THE TITLE BOUT...

IT'S NIA VS HARU IN...

THE TIME TO SCRAP TOURNAMENT CHAMPIONSHIP!!!

Chapter 18. Nia vs Haru! The Time To Scrap Champion!

"From Atlanta Georgia, at 5'6 weighing 135 pounds at 18 years of age, Nia! Power, hair control!"

People chant and roar for her. Master Isaiah and I do too.

"If Nia wins, not only will she be the first black woman to win this, but the first woman in general to win. And the youngest person to ever win! That's big!", Master Isaiah tells me over the loud arena of people.

"And from Tokyo Japan, at 6'2 weighing 181 pounds at 20 years of age, Haru! Power, Ze power!"

People chant for him too. Many Japanese Americans cheer for him and Asians all across the world attend this event and watch from home. Nia has many fans as well, especially with her association with me and Master Isaiah.

"Now this is for the championship!!!", the announcer yells as fans get more hype. Many people with Japan flags and American flags and ATL hats show their support. A lot of celebrities show up as well, especially rappers from Atlanta and New York.

"Now…. IT'S TIME TO SCRAP!!!", the announcer yells as the crowd irrupts.

They both get into their stance. The crowd goes back and forth chanting Haru and Nia. They circle around each other to size each other up. You can feel the tension between them two just by how they stare at each other. Both know that everything is on the line. All the training, all the pain, and all the sacrifices, all on the line tonight.

I still wish it was me in the championship fight, but I know it'll still be worth it if Nia wins tonight. Hell, it already is.

"Haru! Now!", Jiro yells.

"Ze Power!!!", Haru yells as he throws a Ze blast.

Me and Master Isaiah yells for her to dodge, but she does easily. Haru throws more and more but Nia dodges them all.

"You're going to have to do more than that to beat me! I mean…. how could you lose…. especially since you've been using Khaos!", she yells.

Haru and Jiro both get a look of surprise on their face, like they've been caught stealing money from the bank. The crowd freezes and so does me and Master Isaiah. We didn't expect her to straight up expose them both on the spot like that.

"Wow, Nia is gangster!", I say to myself.

Haru, in rage and in anger, swings and uppercuts Nia. The punch is so powerful, you can see the Ze smoke trail the punch and Nia falls on the complete other side of the mat. She struggles to get up.

"You shut your mouth girl!", Haru yells.

People start to boo him and some even chant Khaos to mock him. He yells at the crowd to shut up and they boo him even more.

"Haru! End this NOW!", Jiro demands.

Haru yells and charges towards Nia on the ground but she whips him off his feet with her hair. The crowd cheers for her. She then wraps her hair around Haru's neck.

"Give up!!!", she yells.

She holds them there for a little while, but I see his eyes turn white. He yells and releases a Ze Power aura and it knocks Nia back. Blood starts streaming from the top of her head down her face.

Haru yells and throws more Ze blasts, but Nia dodges, flips, and ducks under them. She then with her hair wraps her hair around both of Haru's wrist. Haru sees this and yanks his arms to him, dragging Nia towards him and he head buds her. He then punches her over and over and over again with Ze. He pauses and Nia tries to connect a punch desperately but Haru dodges and swings again and knocks her to the ground.

The boo's get louder and people chant for Nia to rise, trying to stomach this gruesome beat down.

Nia stumbles up, but as soon as she does, Haru hits her with another blast attack. Nia falls out on the ground cold. People boo and some even throw drinks and food.

"NIA!!!", I shout. "GET UP!!!"

Her eyes open and she barely gets up at two.

Her face is very bloody, and I know she took at least thirty punches. The crowd starts to chant and roar Nia's name. She gets back into her stance.

"Stay down!!!", Haru yells in anger.

He runs towards her again and punches her with Ze again. She flops back and spits out a lot of blood. As he runs towards her again, she whips him in the eye with her hair. He stumbles back and yells in pain.

The crowd gets hype again. Seeing this, Nia hits him in the other eye, and he stumbles back and rubs them.

"Nice one Nia!", Master Isaiah yells.

She yells and wraps her hair around his arms again and gets close to him. She spreads his arms apart as far as she can with the back two braids. And with her front two braids she spreads his legs so he can't hit her back. Then she punches Haru in his stomach, chest, and face with all she's got. He's defenseless and can't do anything to stop it.

"She's smart as hell!", Master Isaiah yells.

"What a move by Nia!", one of the commentators yell.

Haru, with desperation, head buds her again.

Nia, while shaken, doesn't let go, and yells and kicks him, right where... well every guy has one week spot, and she kicks him there, very hard.

He yells very loudly, and the crowd all cringe, as if they could feel it too. She lets go of him but falls as well. She holds her head in pain.

"That shouldn't be legal!!!", one commentator says visibly irate.

"Well, if he's using Khaos like alleged, then I don't want to hear it! This is the Time to Scrap Tournament!!", the other one says.

They both stumble to their feet, both very bruised and bloody.

"You.... won't.... beat me!", Nia says as she catches her breath.

Haru chuckles. "I've already won. If you know the truth, then you know you can't beat me. So just give up so I don't hurt you anymore girl."

Nia slowly rises her hand and flicks him off. The crowd goes crazy and Haru loses it and rushes towards her in anger.

He throws a lot of punches, but Nia dodges them all and wraps her hair around the back of his head and brings his head down to meet her knees, and knees him twice in the face.

She lets go and spin kicks him.

"Let's go Nia!!!", I shout.

Haru stumbles and when Nia runs to him, he uppercuts her with a Ze Punch again. Before she falls to the ground, he grabs her leg and slams her hard to the mat. The thud can be heard and felt by everyone.

The crowd cringes as they see the impact and Nia lets out a loud yell in pain. Haru waits as Nia struggles to get up, blood leaking from her head down her body. This match is just as bloody as my match with Haru, if not more. It pisses me off watching and I want to beat his ass, but if I do, I'll ruin Nia's chance at winning. She wouldn't want that. I know she's strong, and I know she'll win.

We chant for Nia to rise to her feet, but it doesn't seem she's going to make it. I hear her talking to herself.

"Come on! I…. have to get up!!!"

She looks at me on the side of the mat. I yell for her to get up. She smirks at me and rises to her feet at one. I smirk back at her and the crowd cheers.

Haru has a look of frustration.

"End this now!!!! Haru end it NOW!!!", Jiro yells as the crowd chants Nia.

Her nose is crooked, and she spits out a tooth. She yells and charges at Haru and they trade blows. They punch and dodge, and punch and dodge, and punch and dodge. Haru yells very aggressively and kicks her in the stomach with Ze.

Nia bends over and holds her stomach, but before he can attack again, she does her hair cutter, helicopter like move. A loud pop can be heard throughout the whole arena.

However, that move takes all the energy she has, and she falls when Haru falls.

Me, Master Isaiah, and the whole entire crowd cheer for Nia to rise. Even the people who started off this fight cheering for Haru.

"Six!"

Nothing

"Five!"

Nothing

"Four!"

Nia flinches her arm and somehow, someway, rises to her feet. The crowd pops again as Haru still lies on the ground. Jiro and Akio chant for him to rise.

"Three!"

Nothing

"Two!"

Nothing

"One!"

Haru struggles his body back to his feet and squares up. Nia looks over to me and Master Isaiah in disbelief.

"Joseph! Master Isaiah! I can't! I'll die! My body hurts too bad!", she tells us over the sea of people yelling her name. She's hurt so badly we can barely understand what she's saying.

"Yes you can Nia! You've done it all girl! You got this! Just one more attack! You got this GOAT girl!", Master Isaiah yells.

She smirks a little and nods her head.

"ENOUGH!! THIS IS ENOUGH! END THIS RIGHT NOW HARU! END IT NOW!!! YOU'VE ALREADY DISGRACED US ENOUGH! BEAT HER NOW!!!", Jiro yells.

His veins pop threw his neck and forehead as his face and body turns red. Haru charges up a Ze blast but with both of his hands. I know if Nia gets hit by this, it'll be over.

Nia has a look of worry and hopelessness on her face. She has given up and looks like she has come to terms that she's going to lose.

My eyes open widely as I remember what Nia told me that night I got Ze. About her faith in God, and in herself.

"FAITH NIA!!! IT'S IN ALL OF US! USE IT!!!!", I scream at her.

She still keeps the same look of defeat on her face. She just stares at Haru with an emotionless, painful, bloody face and breathes heavily.

Haru still charges up his Ze blasts and behind him a dragon forms with the white smoke behind him. It's the biggest Ze Blast I've ever seen charged. It's crazy how he still has this much energy, but I guess it's the Khaos.

"THINK ABOUT EVERYONE NIA! THINK ABOUT YOURSELF! YOU'RE SO CLOSE! DO IT!", I scream.

"Amanda. Kaya. Atlanta. Master Isaiah. Regan. Naya.   Nivea.", Nia says to herself.

When she says her sisters name, she begins to cry. She puts both of her hands wide open in front of her face.

"Ok Joseph!! ZE……POWER!!!", she yells as a white glow and smoke starts to form around her.

The crowd gets louder than it's ever been, and the commentators go crazy too. Master Isaiah has a look of disbelief, alongside Haru and Jiro. I smile like a proud parent, or……boyfriend, and cheer her on to do it.

Hers gets way bigger, way faster than Haru does.

"ZE BLAST!!!!!!!", she yells as she releases the blast. It goes quickly across and Haru tries to throw his but it's too late. It explodes right in front of him, causing a big wave of energy threw the arena as people's hair fly back as the wind smacks them directly in the face. It blinds everyone and the white, bright glow and smoke stay for 30 seconds after the collision causing everyone to be blind for a while.

Once the brightness and smoke calms down, we see both Nia and Haru both knocked on the ground. Haru's top half of his robe has been burned off. And Nia's clothes are ripped and burned as well. Both are extremely bloody and so is the mat.

But Nia somehow……. someway…… rises to her knees as the announcer counts down.

And eventually to her feet at one.

"Ladies in gentlemen, your new Time to Scrap Tournament Champion, Nia!!!", the announcer yells.

The crowd goes crazy and chant her name as confetti falls from the ceiling. Nia did it. After all we've been through together. Nia won the Time to Scrap Tournament.

Chapter 19. Two Legends, One Life. What's Next?

I run to Nia's aid and so does Master Isaiah. She falls out flat as soon as the announcer says her name. She doesn't even have enough energy to get her medal and prize money.

"Nia!", I say trying to wake her up. I don't know how she'll hear me over the roar of the crowd.

She's out cold, but I hear and feel her heart beating. I pick her up and hold her in my arms. As I hold her, the crowd starts chanting Joseph and Nia. I look around and notice that Nia and I impacted the tournament and the world, more than just fighting, but overcoming the odds. I put one hand up to wave towards the crowd.

Master Isaiah rushes towards Haru to make sure he's fine along with other medics. It takes them a while, but they eventually get him to his feet. Master Isaiah offers Haru a handshake.

"What are you doing!?", I ask him. "He cheated!"

"Yea, but I know it wasn't his fault Joseph. Jiro got you to do it huh? After you lost the exhibition huh?", Master Isaiah asks Haru.

He puts his head down in shame while Jiro glances at Master Isaiah. He glances back though.

"Haru, you're a man of honor. You could never win while neglecting your principles. Could you?", Master Isaiah ask. Haru nods his head no. Jiro snickers.

"Yea, because he is weak. I was able to do what I had to do. That's why I won and was able to beat you Isaiah!", Jiro says.

Master Isaiah looks around at me and Nia. He then looks around the crowd, soaking the moment in. All this, including me and Nia, stems from him and he knows he won in spirit. Jiro looks at the roaring crowd too. People cry tears of joy for Nia's win and it's an overall, good feeling moment. Their eyes both meet each other again.

Master Isaiah chuckles and says, "No, I won Jiro."

Jiro with anger spits on the ground.

"I'll be back in four years, with someone way stronger than both of them! My true fighter!"

He yanks Akio towards Master Isaiah. "You can have them both! They're weak! Just wait my friend. Just you wait."

Akio tries to charge Jiro, but Master Isaiah holds him back. "We'll be waiting. And we'll be stronger.", Master Isaiah says.

Jiro smirks.

"And that's a promise!", I say.

Jiro glances at me with a face of disgust. He turns around and walks out the arena.

"Jo…. Joseph?", Nia says as she starts to wake up.

"Shhhhh.", I say. "Save your breath. We're on our way to the hospital.", I tell her.

"Thank you.", she says. She falls back out cold.

We leave and take Nia and Haru to the hospital.

Two Months Later

It's been two months since the fight. Nia and Haru have been in the hospital in New York but today Haru is cleared to leave. Before he leaves, he offers me a handshake.

"Fool me once, shame on you. Fool me twice, shame on me.", I say.

"Fine.", he says. He then grabs my arm and pulls me in for a hug. I'm shocked and don't understand. He lets go of me.

"I apologize for my dishonor. I also thank you and Master Isaiah for bringing me here for aid. Lastly, tell Master Isaiah thanks for allowing me and my cousin to train with him. When we get home, we'll transfer here for some time."

"Oh, no problem Haru. Also be ready, Master Isaiah doesn't play around with his training.", I say.

"Are you participating in the next tournament Joseph?", he asks.

"I'll have to see. But if I do, just know you won't get better than me."

He smirks and walks off. I ask one more thing before he leaves.

"Haru! Why did you save me in Memphis if you didn't like me?"

He grins. "Who said I didn't like you? Plus, I don't think even Jiro is that low to watch people die, I hope. Be ready though, he'll train someone to beat us both down."

"Ok.", I respond.

"Also, I couldn't have gotten my rematch if you were dead, now could I?", he says.

"Wowww! Jeez thanks pal.", I say sarcastically.

He chuckles and walks out the hospital. I still don't know much about Haru, but I feel like I've made a new friend, or at least a new rival. I can't wait to train with him, Nia, and Akio if I decide to fight again.

Two weeks later, Nia clears herself out the hospital. We offer to take her home. She's already helped Kaya and Amanda with some of her prize money while she was in the hospital. We get on our plane, and I notice the captain say something and it raises my anxiety.

"Trip to Memphis is ready."

"Wait…this is to Memphis? I thought it was Atlanta I say out loud. Nia grabs me and sits me down.

"What? What's the problem? We have to get you to Atlanta.", I say.

"Look, I was going to surprise you, but... I bought a new house for your mom and sister."

"Really?!", I ask in excitement.

"Everything ok sir? Is this your flight?", the pilot asks me.

"Oh, yes. Sorry about that." He walks away.

"Are you freaking kidding me Nia. You took care of my mom and sister?! You didn't have to do that, it was your prize money…", I say before she interrupts and puts a finger in front of my mouth.

"It's ok. I wouldn't have won without you. I figured I could help others with my money, and you most definitely helped me. I gave up in those final moments, but you put the faith back in me.", she says.

We both smile and blush at each other.

"Good to know I get no credit for neither one of you.", Master Isaiah says in a seat right behind us.

"Of course Master, this is all possible because of you.", I say.

"Yea, thank you. Sincerely.", Nia says.

"Yea, better thank me. Also, stop with the flirting. I kind of view you two as my kids, so stop making this weird.", he jokes.

"You know, I can still hook you up with someone if you want me to Master Isaiah.", Nia jokes back.

"Yep, I'm going to kick both of your asses when we get off this plane."

"What did I do?", I ask.

We all laugh.

We land in Memphis and go pick up my mother and sister. Before they can ask questions or talk to me about the tournament, we get them in the car.

"Where are we going boy?", my momma asks.

"You'll see, watch.", I say trying to hide the happiness in my voice. I can tell I'm failing though, and I sense that they know something is up.

Master Isaiah drives us while we follow Nia to the house. Savannah is with Nia though, but we have Bishop, who's shaking because he's not used to being inside a car. I guess with all this fighting stuff I totally forgot about normal things like learning how to drive.

We eventually make it to the house and even I'm blown away. It's in the beautiful suburbs and is a nice size house. My mom breaks down into tears as we pull into the driveway. The tears continue as we enter the house.

"Nia, you didn't have to.", she starts.

"Yes I did ma'am. Joseph helped me a lot, this is the least I could do.", Nia replies.

We enter the house and are amazed by all the nice luxuries the house has to offer. Bishop runs around the house with the zoomies. Even Master Isaiah is blown away. Nia notices his face.

"You know if you want a new house, I can get you one too Master.", she says.

"No thank you. You gave me all I needed when you won the tournament. I'm very proud of you.", he says. She tries to hold back tears but can't. Master Isaiah walks up to her and gives her a hug.

I go to search for an extra room. There is three of them, but one of them is already furnished with bonus room things, like a pool table and air hockey.

"Where's my room?", I ask.

"What do you mean, your room?", Savannah mocks

"My room dummy.", I mock back.

"Well, yours is down the street, DUMMY. I thought Nia told you.", Savannah says.

I look at her with so much confusion on my face. Then I take my face of confusion towards Nia, whose smirking at me in the corner of the living room.

"What is she talking about Nia?", I ask.

"Well, I thought about it and well, I decided that with my sister being gone and my parents being my parents, there isn't much left for me in Atlanta. So, I moved my family down here as well and, well, hoped that you would want to live with me down the street in the house I bought for us.", she says.

"Us? You mean, like, live together? In one house?", I say as I try to get the words out. I'm so surprised and shocked and it feels like a fantasy.

"What else boy?", my momma says. "Go on, that's one less mouth I have to feed."

They all laugh.

I wave them goodbye, and we drive a few blocks over to Nia's……. our new house. As we arrive, it's so beautiful that I can't actually believe this is real. We enter the house to see Regan, Naya, and Regan's family in the living room, Nia's aunt and uncle and their other son. She tells me that her aunt is going to watch Naya, but we'll keep her sometimes too.

We all talk and catch up. Her family really likes me too. They loved my fights and mostly my speech. Nia even jokes that they may like me more than they like her.

As everyone leaves, Nia goes to put Naya to sleep, and I help her. We both enter the living room to see Master Isaiah knocked out asleep on the long couch. We both plow down on the loveseat.

"This is so much Nia. I can't thank you enough.", I say.

"It's the least I could do.", she says.

She then moves her hair and ties it around my feet and yanks me off the couch. I fall and she bursts out into laughter.

"Never mind. I can thank you enough.", I say jokingly.

"It's a joke. Calm down big baby. She uses her hair and pulls me to her, and we kiss.

"That's why I did this. I love you Joseph.", she tells me.

"I love you too Nia.", I respond. We kiss again.

"Sooo, will we be back for the next fight?", she asks.

"Most likely. But next time, I'm winning.", I tell her.

"Hmph, sure you will. Like I told you before, I'll win and you can try to come in second.", she says. We both laugh.

You know, after all I've been through, everything seems worth it in the end now. If someone would have told me that this would have been my life when I was getting jumped by No Games and Red Angel, I would've laughed in their face. Or looked at them like they were stupid. But now I see the truth of what the right mindset, the right amount of ambition and passion, and what the right people around you can do.

I've grown up and spent most of my life so far in hell. Lost my dad to the cops in front of me. Had a gun pointed at me more than once. And lived through the harsh life of poverty with my mom, sister, and my dog. I've worked since I was 14 to even attempt to help my mom with food, keep the lights on, and so many other hard tasks. And when all seemed lost, I turned to something that some would say would be impossible for me to win. The Time to Scrap Tournament.

But with faith, and Master Isaiah and Nia and so many others, I've come a long way. And even though I didn't win, I came out on top. And I'm not alone up here either.

Maybe I'll enter the tournament again. Not for my own personal gain, but to help others in situations just like mines, or worse.

But for now, me and Nia live our lives happily, as…

Two legends….

One Life.

The End…

Well, that would be the end if some big ass man named Mr. USA didn't come knocking on our door so hard that it falls. Me and Nia both jump up in fear.

"What the hell is wrong with you!", Nia says. "I just bought this house!"

"I see, nice place you got. Also, you two look so cute.", he says.

"How did you find us?", I ask.

"That doesn't matter! But what does matter is you two better be ready and ready fast! We're going to need you both!", he says.

"We? Whose we?", Nia asks.

"And for what?", I jump in.

"Jiro is already up to no good. And if the rumors are true, then it could be way worse than some tournament beef. Also, "we", are me, Austin U.K., Kaya, and Magic Moses. We're in the process of recruiting more fighters!", he says in his country voice.

"Just tell us what's going on USA?", Nia asks.

"Jiro is helping Mr. Russia with a plan to dominate the, the world to simply put it, and we need you two badly! Also only call me Mr. USA, USA by itself just sounds weird.", he says.

Me and Nia both look at each other in disbelief.

"We can never catch a break.", I tell her.

She agrees.

"Fine Mr. USA, we're in, but what's next", I ask.

"We go to Japan in a few weeks with the others, be ready to truly scrap. Lives are on the line now.", he says.

"Well with Ze Power and Hair Control, I think we got all we need.", Nia says.

"Yea, but first I need to have a little talk with the tournament officials about Khoas.", I say.

"We'll do that along the way.", Mr. USA says.

We all smile, as we prepare for our next journey and mission in life, and where our faith takes us next.

Okay The End For Real Now

For Now…

Steadman's Message to You!

Hello lucky reader! Thank you for reading my first book, Time to Scrap! Before I give an update and a brief rundown on things, I would like to thank people who have helped me on this path! PLEASE DON'T SKIP!!!!!!!!!!!!!! IF you've read this much you can read a little bit more lol.

Most importantly I want to thank God for everything he has done for me. For showing a path in life I would have never thought was possible for someone like me. For giving me the heart and ambition to get up and write. For giving me a stable home and life and even when things weren't good, he helped guide me and my family. I still have a lot to learn and try to improve myself every day, but I know he's proud.

I want to thank my mother who has supported me through this unknown journey and being willing to make sacrifices for me. Not just with getting my first book done, but in life in general. I wouldn't be the man I am and becoming without her.

I want to thank my stepfather for helping me on my journey as well and pushing me toward other things in life. And for bringing the family up with his sense of humor.

I want to thank my brother for being my partner in crime when it comes to making these types of stories. Although we both have different plans and future companies and brands planned, I know we will collaborate in the future.

I want to thank my father, sister, aunts, cousins, uncles, grandparents, friends, and anyone who supported me through life and supported my odd dreams of being an author. (May not be odd to you, but for us it is.)

Special thanks to Angie Thomas for showing me that I can be a black author and talk about black problems. To LeBron James for being a perfect example of a strong, ambitious, black man, but also a family man and someone who isn't afraid to speak out against injustices. To Tupac for being a role model and someone with a strong mind. To Kendrick, XXXTENTACION, Ice Cube, Jay-Z and many more artist. And lastly to all my favorite Youtubers. I know it may sound weird, but they inspire and can lift up my day whenever I'm down or even depressed. So thanks to Markiplier, CoryxKenshin, IBerleezy and the entire eezy gang, and lastly RDCworld1. There are so many other celebrities and influencers who I look up to and can thank, but I don't want to be here all day. (I'm literally typing this in class when I should be doing my essay.)

And last but not least, I WANT TO THANK YOU!!! Thank you so much for reading my book. I really hoped you enjoyed my book, and the future ones I have planned.

Speaking of that… be on the lookout for future books from me. I plan to do mostly comics/manga books, but there will be a few other traditional books as well. And an important hint…make sure you got every detail from this book. You may see it again somewhere else. Once again… thank you all.

You can follow me on Instagram and soon Twitter for more upcoming news and updates.

Instagram: steadman_entertainment

Personal Account: steadxman

P.S: I Know my names are stupid! That's why I need to get verified! Stop laughing!

From Chris Steadman.

© Copyright Claim, 2021, Christopher Steadman.

All rights reserved. Under no circumstances may be used nor copied. No plagiarism of any kind from this book and can only be quoted in reviews.

Made in the USA
Coppell, TX
17 March 2022